A CINDERELLA RETELLING

DAMNATION

A TALE OF CINDER
BOOK 3

M.J. HAAG

ISBN 978-1-943051-22-9 (eBook Edition)
ISBN 978-1-943051-33-5 (CreateSpace Paperback Edition)
ISBN 978-1-943051-24-3 (Paperback Edition)

The characters and events in this book are fictitious. Any similar to real persons, living or dead, is coincidental and not intended by the author.

Editing by Ulva Eldridge
Cover design by Shattered Glass Publishing LLC

To my grandma and my mom, thanks for giving me the writing bug.
You'll be missed, grandma.

DAMNATION

Abused but not beaten, I will break the curse.

With the reason behind her mother's death revealed, it's a race for Eloise to exact her revenge and prevent her stepsisters from marrying the prince. However, amidst the glittering jewels and colorful ballgowns, the royal court holds secrets of its own that will devastate Eloise and strike a final blow to her plans. Betrayed by the one person she thought she could trust, Eloise questions how far she's willing to go for revenge.

After all, in the game of kingdoms, everyone is a pawn.

CHAPTER ONE

My stomach growled loudly, waking me. With a groan, I rolled to my back and winced as the chain holding me to the fireplace rattled loudly in the quiet of the kitchen.

As much as I dreaded Maeve's return, I hoped she would hurry.

I had no doubt she had sensed her mirror's destruction the moment it happened. And given that I'd attempted to break it once before, there was no question that I would be the one punished despite the manacle still securely wrapped around my wrist. However, while I knew Maeve would enter this home in a fury, I didn't fear her arrival. She couldn't hurt me, not truly.

No, I needed Maeve to return so I could hear what had become of Kellen. I thought of her, fast asleep somewhere, unable to prevent whatever Maeve had planned with her cursed apple. There was nothing I could do but fear for my sister's fate.

Sighing, I sat up and threw a log onto the embers. What would have happened if I hadn't witnessed Maeve with Hugh and her use of the amulet? Would Kellen and I still be together and safe, or would something more terrible have happened to us? Would all those innocent people still have died? I thought of Judith, Anne, and Mother and felt a bitter pang of longing.

Nothing could change the past. The choices I'd made were irrevocable, and I would need to face the choices yet to come. And, it was those future choices that plagued my thoughts continuously. What should I do when Maeve returned? Should I acknowledge I'd broken her mirror or feign innocence? What would best serve my purpose to prevent one of my stepsisters from wedding the prince? Round and round went my thoughts.

The dining room door opened, and Porcia walked in.

"Good morning, Eloise," she said cordially. "Did you sleep well?"

"I haven't been fed more than a crust of bread since Mama left, and I've slept chained to the hearth. What answer do you think I can honestly give?"

"One that's dishonest," she said, meeting my gaze. "Have you learned nothing?"

There was no anger in the question. In fact, there was little emotion at all. In that moment, she reminded me of myself whenever I spoke to Maeve.

"I've always struggled at being an adept student," I said.

"Then your suffering has only just begun," she said.

Turning her back on me, she grabbed her cloak and went outside to collect eggs. A task I used to perform. One I desperately wanted to return to. I hated all of the time I'd been forced to spend indoors. If not for the uncertainty of the spell binding me to the estate, I might have tried to run instead of waiting here, chained like an animal. I gave my manacle an angry tug.

Cecilia took that moment to enter the dining room and let out a laugh.

"Do you honestly think you can free yourself? It's more than metal holding you in place. It's a curse. And no one's magic is stronger than Mama's."

Playing my role, I glared at her then turned to stare at the flames slowly licking their way up the log.

"Perhaps I made a mistake in feeding you yesterday," Cecilia said, sounding too much like Maeve. "Another day of hunger should make you more docile for Mama's return tomorrow."

I looked at Cecilia.

"Do you think that if I'm suitably starved beside the fire, Mama will praise you for your cleverness?" I asked. "Don't be daft. She's going to be upset. By your very own words, she wants me alive to witness her triumph."

Cecilia's eyes narrowed on me.

"I'm willing to risk her wrath to see you suffer."

Porcia entered the kitchen and removed her cloak.

"Good morning, sister. There are fresh eggs for breakfast as well as the stale bread you left on the table yesterday."

Cecilia's angry gaze swung to her sister, checking for any hint of reproach. Porcia remained focused on placing the eggs in a pot filled with water before carrying it to me.

"Place this on the fire, Eloise, and tell me when the water boils."

Without argument, I hung the pot over the flames because I knew doing so would annoy Cecilia.

"We should go to town as soon as we've eaten," Porcia said, joining her sister at the table. "With so many in Towdown now ill, we may not find a seamstress who can complete a dress for each of us in time for the ball. Finding one shop with two gowns already premade might be our only option."

"I agree. If we want the best selection—"

"Then you should have looked yesterday," I said. "The moment you saw the proclamation."

Cecilia glared at me, and I smiled. We both knew I was correct.

A noise rose, faint at first but growing louder.

"A rider," Cecilia said.

The thunder of hooves outside abruptly stopped. Porcia rose to see who it might be; but before she crossed half the room, the door flew open.

Maeve stormed into the kitchen, still disguised as the old crone. Her cloudy gaze swept the room, noting her daughters then me. I didn't miss the lingering look she gave the manacle circling my wrist. Just as I didn't miss the extra dirt that now clung to her clothes or the new rips to her garments. Whatever Maeve had done hadn't been easy.

"Mama," Porcia said in shock. "We weren't expecting you for another day."

Maeve lashed out, striking her daughter across the face.

"Do not speak," she said in her deep, grating voice.

Porcia lifted her hand to hold her cheek then thought better of it and clasped her hands in front of herself instead. Cecilia remained at the table, wisely not speaking as she warily watched her mother. Not that Maeve noticed.

She remained focused on me as a pulse of green light started at her chest. The glow grew larger and brighter with each beat until the emerald radiance enveloped her. The lines on her face smoothed, and her hair darkened as signs of her false age disappeared. Slowly, she straightened to her full height before the light faded away once more. But not from her eyes. The glow remained there as she studied me, her face flushed with anger.

I didn't consciously make my choice before words tumbled from my mouth in a rush.

"I didn't mean to kill Hugh, and I swear never to touch your mirror again. I vow I'll be a proper young lady. Please, Mama. I'll do as you ask if only you allow me to eat."

Her gaze narrowed on me, and my stomach took that moment to growl loudly. She looked at Porcia then Cecilia.

"Come with me," she said.

She strode from the room without another glance in my direction.

As soon as the door closed behind Porcia, I exhaled slowly and looked around me. Blame could still be cast in my direction if Maeve thought for a moment I'd escaped my bond. She would need proof that I hadn't. Pretending ignorance about any knowledge of the mirror's destruction wouldn't be enough.

Thinking quickly, I lay on the floor and stretched out to my full length, once again trying to reach for the broom. My breathing quiet in comparison to my pulse, I struggled to listen for sounds of their approach. The door swung open again just as my shoulder cracked from the strain of pulling against the manacle.

I sat up in a rush and guiltily met Maeve's scrutiny.

"What were you doing?" she asked.

Not needing to feign nervousness, my gaze flicked to Cecilia and Porcia. Cecilia's face was now as red as Porcia's.

Getting to my feet, I focused on Maeve.

"I was trying to get the broom. I thought I might be able to knock the bread from the table."

She tilted her head at me.

"When was the last time you fed your sister, Cecilia?"

"Last night."

"What did you feed her?" she asked without looking away from me.

"A crust of bread," Cecilia answered.

"Does Eloise look hungry to you?"

Cecilia glared at me.

"It had to be her, Mama. She's feigning her—"

Maeve pivoted so quickly that I heard the crack of her hand against Cecilia's cheek before noting her arm had moved.

"Can you make your stomach growl on command? You admitted to me that you spent time away from the estate. If she could free herself, would she not eat?" She pointed to the tray. "Was there any food missing?"

"We didn't check the cellar," Cecilia said defiantly.

"Check. And if everything is accounted for, you will pay for your incompetence with your blood."

"And Porcia?" Cecilia dared ask.

"Your sister never tried to claim competence greater than Eloise's, did she?"

With a nod, Cecilia went to the cellar. Maeve turned toward me.

"What happened while they were gone?" she asked.

I studied her for a quiet moment and saw that a hint of glow remained in her eyes.

"I tried to reach the broom. When that didn't work, I screamed long and loud. Then, I stared at the fire until I heard Porcia and Cecilia return."

"Did anyone come?"

I shook my head. "No, Mama."

"My mirror is destroyed, Eloise. What do you have to say?"

"Ah." I glanced at the fire for a moment before meeting

her gaze. "How?"

"That seems to be the mystery, doesn't it? My bedroom door was locked, and you were chained in the kitchen. Despite that, Cecilia believes it was you who broke the mirror."

"As I've tried destroying it in the past, I can understand why. However, I tried breaking it because I feared you were going to use it to hurt Kellen. Why break it after you'd already left to..." I looked at the floor, truly unable to speak for several moments.

"Is she still alive?" I asked finally.

"She is," Maeve said.

Relief filled me only to leave just as quickly. Alive didn't mean safe.

"What did you do to her?" I asked, meeting her gaze.

Maeve's eyes hardened.

"I ensured she would be no threat to our plans to win the prince's affection."

My heart chilled at those words. *Yes*, I thought sadly. *Alive most assuredly did not mean safe.* Irrationally, I wished I hadn't destroyed the mirror so I could look upon my sister.

Footsteps heralded Cecilia's return. When she emerged from the cold storage, her face was pale.

"Everything is still there," she said.

"Go out to the shed. Find a lash. Don't stop until I come for you."

Cecilia nodded stiffly and started for the door.

"Mama," Porcia said hesitantly. "Perhaps Cecilia's

punishment should wait until after we visit the dressmaker."

Maeve looked at her youngest daughter.

"Explain."

"A proclamation was made that there is to be a ball tomorrow evening to celebrate the Prince's return." She held her hand out to Cecilia.

Cecilia took the proclamation from her bodice and gave it to her sister. Porcia quickly handed it to Maeve.

"Cecilia and I were just about to leave for town to find gowns. We didn't want to wait too long or we might have difficulty obtaining the best."

Maeve unfolded the paper and read through it, a slow smile curving her lips.

"The mirror's loss will not go unpunished. However, your reason for staying that punishment is sound, my dear one. It wouldn't do to stir gossip immediately before the ball." She looked at Cecilia. "The evening we return from the ball, you will take the lashings for your incompetence in safeguarding the oldest and most trusted means we had to watch our quarry. Use this extra time wisely. Find proof that it was your sister."

Maeve glanced at me.

"Meanwhile, feed her. I will not have her die needlessly." She turned and started for the dining room. "I must change and clean up my room. We will leave for town immediately afterward."

In the silence following her departure, Cecilia took her sister's hand.

"Thank you," she said. "I will not forget your kindness when I am queen. Feed the bitch for me. I need to find proof of her guilt."

"Of course," Porcia said.

Cecilia swept from the room without a look at me.

"The eggs, Eloise," Porcia said.

I used my skirt to pull the pot from the fire and set it on the hearth. Porcia took it from there and removed the eggs with a spoon. She gave me two along with bread and water.

"Eat while you can. Cecilia will find something. Have no doubt."

Overhead, something banged loudly, followed by several more crashes.

I frowned and ate my food. The noise continued long after I finished. When Maeve returned to the kitchen, she barely spared the ceiling a glance as she uncuffed me.

"Wash," she said.

Gratefully, I hurried outside to do as she commanded. I couldn't help but wish I had time for a full bath, though, instead of a quick swipe of a cloth at the trough outside.

Under Maeve's watchful eyes, I removed the soot from my skin and shook out my skirt.

"Don't bother," she said. "You'll change before we leave."

Her words caught my attention. Leave? Did that mean I

was to go to town with them? I was so occupied with my thoughts that I didn't notice the silence inside.

"Mama!" Cecilia's shout rang out.

Looking up, I saw her leaning out an open window above, joy in her expression. In her hands, she held several papers and a familiar book. My heart froze, and my stomach wanted to expel my long-awaited breakfast.

"I found many items of interest in Eloise's room," she said before disappearing inside.

"Come, Eloise. Let us see if your sister has spared herself her lashings."

I followed Maeve inside, never more grateful for Rose's spell that kept me safe from physical harm.

"It's a spell book," Cecilia said, entering the kitchen moments after we did. "And letters from a caster named Elspeth." She held out the book and a pile of letters in one hand. In the other was a single folded piece of parchment.

"What is that?" Maeve asked.

"A letter from Kellen to Eloise. Proof that Eloise knew about the book and those letters." She gave the letters to Maeve. She read Kellen's letter first. Then, without looking up, she started reading the letters to Mother from Elspeth. Her face grew redder with each one, and the light started to pulse at her chest. When she finished, she gave the book the barest of glances.

"I knew your mother hadn't acted alone," Maeve said softly. She looked up, and her eyes glinted with a hard, green light.

"You knew of these letters, and you never told me?" She stood and slowly walked toward me. "Was it Elspeth who cast the spell of protection on you?"

I opened my mouth to deny it but choked on the words from the second spell Rose cast on me.

Maeve tilted her head to study me.

"What letter does your sister have?" she asked.

I swallowed hard and briefly thought of lying, but something in Maeve's eyes told me she already knew. As Kellen had said in her letter, Maeve had been searching for something.

"A letter from the King stating Margaret Cartwright had permission to live at the estate, and that should she or her children ever have need, they could call upon him."

Maeve halted before me, unmoving, gaze unfocused. I waited, ignoring the growing smile on Cecilia's face as she remained behind Maeve.

"Your sister is a disappointment to me, and I do not regret my decision to leave her where she is, out of our way." A secretive smile lifted Maeve's lips. "Eating the apple will ensure no Prince will touch her now. However, what am I to do with you?" She began to circle me and flicked my dirty hair. "Your deception cannot go unpunished. While you may not have broken the mirror, I cannot help but think you had a part in planning its destruction."

She stopped before me.

"I cannot hurt you, but I can hurt others while you watch."

I said nothing and kept my face perfectly blank.

"I know how losing Heather and Catherine pained you. I think perhaps it's time we found new help."

My chest tightened at the thought. How many more deaths would I have to witness?

"There's no need," I said. "I'm happy to cook and clean for you."

Maeve smiled knowingly.

"What a sweet, self-sacrificing offer. Would you still be so willing if I were to host a dinner party tonight to celebrate the Prince's impending return?"

My stomach once again threatened to empty. I swallowed hard and remembered all of the things that Catherine and Heather had to do. Would I be able to endure such acts to spare others from having to endure them? My hands trembled.

Maeve's grin widened.

"I thought not. However, your suggestion has merit. For now, I will allow you to serve as a maid. If you perform your duties—washing, cooking, cleaning—then I will not need to bring any other maids here."

"Yes, Mama."

"However," she said, turning to look at Cecilia, "we will need more than a maid if we're to keep up appearances. Go to town and find a new man for us. Someone without family or ties to town. Someone like Hugh."

"Yes, Mama." Cecilia dipped her head and started toward the door.

"Cecilia," Maeve said, stopping her daughter just as she reached the door. "Don't mistake your paltry discovery as evidence to deflect blame for your failure. Whether broken by Eloise or some caster our dear Eloise has managed to find, it was your responsibility to protect the mirror. You will make amends."

"Yes, Mama."

Maeve smiled at Cecilia.

"I think the docks would be a suitable place to find the help we need. Remember, it must be someone passing through with no ties to the people in town. And, be sure to measure his 'worth' before returning. I will not settle for anything less than Hugh's measure." Maeve gave a sigh. "That man was magnificent in bed."

I shuddered slightly as Cecilia nodded once more and left.

Maeve's gaze pinned me.

"Prepare a bath. I'm sure whoever she finds will need a thorough washing before he's fit to serve us. And prepare something to eat. Impress me, Eloise, or I will bring others into this house who will."

CHAPTER TWO

NAKED AND UNASHAMED, THE MAN STOOD BEFORE US IN THE kitchen. Although I kept my gaze firmly on his face, my cheeks felt as if I had sat too close to a roaring fire.

Maeve circled him like a wolf circled prey. This new man was much like Hugh in build and handsome enough to look upon once the salt was washed from his skin and hair. Maeve seemed to think so, too, as she ran a finger along his skin while the firelight glinted off the water still on his tall, lean frame. A small smile played about his mouth like he found her amusing.

I pitied him. Yet, there was little I could do to prevent what was to come. I'd already tried to warn him away when I'd brought him a rinse bucket.

"Are you sure you want to give up your life at sea to work on an estate run by a woman?"

"A life at sea can be very lonely, and your daughter was

very persuasive that sinking my roots here would be worth my while."

Maeve chuckled.

"I do hope you are willing to sink your roots deeply, for I require absolute loyalty. Can you swear to give me that?"

He boldly lifted a hand and touched Maeve's cheek.

"You're a very fine woman." He glanced at the three of us. "You all are. I'd gladly service all of you."

Maeve captured his hand.

"Those are my daughters," she said, losing her humor. "You've met Cecilia. Beside her is Porcia. Behind them is Eloise. You will not touch any of them. It will be only me you serve."

"Aye, I can swear to give you my loyalty while you desire it."

"What is your name?"

"Seth, My Lady."

"I will take you into my service, Seth."

A green light flared and was absorbed into his soft brown eyes.

"Come," Maeve said. "Let us seal our pact in privacy."

His grin widened, and with a heavy heart, I watched them leave the room.

Cecilia turned to me.

"Eloise, drain the tub, and refill it for me with what remains of the potion. That man's seed is making me itch. He probably had the pox before Mama cleansed him."

She said it all with annoyance, not noting my shock.

Everything Maeve had said about worth and measure suddenly made sense. Cecilia had lured the man here with her own body, and Maeve would ensure he stayed with the use of hers. I'd already witnessed the obsession that developed because of it.

I thought of poor Hugh, dead less than a week, and realized I no longer grieved him. I barely grieved Mother or Father anymore, either. Was I growing used to losing everyone? Even thoughts of Kellen, gone so long now, didn't cause me the same degree of anguish they once had. Was it perhaps because I'd finally realized how little control I had over my situation? Or, was my determination to stop Maeve hardening my heart against all of the people around me who were yet destined for damnation?

As I worked to empty the tub, I decided the reason didn't matter. I was grateful I no longer felt such deep sorrow. Detachment from the suffering of those around me would make it easier to do what I must.

Cecilia started stripping the moment I emptied the last clean bucket of water into the tub.

"Go straighten our rooms," she ordered as Porcia stepped forward to help her.

Leaving the kitchen, I went upstairs to tidy their rooms. The faint sound of low groans emanated from Maeve's chamber, and I hurried through my tasks so I could escape to my attic refuge.

However, what once had been a haven as much as a prison now lay in ruins. My walls were no more. Furniture rested in tumbled heaps across the large expanse. Smaller items, strewn about haphazardly, added to the disarray and made walking through the mess difficult. I picked up an old dress as I made my way toward where my sitting area had been. I wasn't sure if the gown was Mother's or something that was left here before we'd moved in.

Finding a chair, I righted it then sat and looked at the wreckage for a moment. Cecilia had vented her anger at me thoroughly. Not that it had saved her. I smiled a little at the thought of Maeve's words. Cecilia would be punished because I'd succeeded.

It didn't bother me that the attic lay in ruins. I'd made it a haven once and could easily do so again. Perhaps a bit more securely this time.

I'd only managed to clear a small path when I heard Maeve call me from below. I hurried down the stairs and found her waiting for me by the door.

"Seth is bringing the carriage around. It's time to go."

"Yes, Mama."

She held out her hand to me; and I moved toward her, eager to see how she would reverse her spell confining me to the estate. As soon as her hand closed around mine, I felt the tingle of her magic worm its way under my skin.

"Cross the boundaries of the estate at my side, and to me you will be tied."

She smiled at me and released my hand.

"Come let us see if that does the trick." She opened the door and ushered me outside. "Start walking to town."

Curious as to what she'd done, I started down the drive. I knew the moment I crossed the boundary of the estate. Something tugged at my middle, a nauseating twist that demanded I go back. My steps slowed.

"Keep going," Maeve called. I glanced back at her. She didn't stand by the carriage but several feet behind me.

I tried taking another step away from her and the nausea intensified.

"I'll help you," she said. Then she turned and walked back to the carriage. Each step brought an increased level of upset to my stomach.

Understanding her spell, I hurried after her. As soon as I crossed through the boundary, the feeling of sickness vanished.

Maeve said nothing as I climbed into the carriage and sat across from Porcia and Cecilia. Cecilia watched me with a knowing smile that quickly vanished when Maeve took the seat beside me.

"Won't it look odd for a servant to ride with us, Mama?" Cecilia asked.

"It will. But this is one exception to appearances I will allow. Despite her many flaws, Eloise is still my daughter. As are you. I will never give up on my children."

She turned to me.

"However, you will learn to obey."

"Yes, Mama."

The carriage lurched forward, and I watched out the window as we passed the spot where I'd stood. Nothing happened, and I exhaled slowly. If Maeve was with me, I would be able to leave the estate without repercussion. Yet, I would be bound to her side. Such a spell would certainly impede my efforts in finding a way to stop Maeve and my stepsisters from achieving their plans.

The ride through town was eerily quiet. Few people walked the streets. Even the market district was surprisingly barren with many of the vendor stalls empty.

"My prince had better hurry, or we won't have much of a kingdom left to rule," Cecilia said.

"They are ill, not dying," Maeve said. "Our subjects will be fine once the Prince returns."

The carriage pulled to a stop before the seamstress who had been used the last time dresses were required, but the sign before the door stated the shop was closed due to illness.

"Mama, we might have to cure the people we need," Porcia said.

Maeve turned her carefully composed face to her daughter.

"Sweetling, we have our distance from Towdown to explain our continued good health. However, if the people who help us are suddenly cured, do you not believe we will be questioned as the cause?"

Porcia flushed.

"I apologize for speaking without due consideration."

"Thank you," Maeve said. She looked out the window at Seth, who'd hopped down for direction from Maeve.

"Continue to drive around until you find a seamstress who is still amenable to work."

"Yes, My Lady."

Moments after he reclaimed his seat, the carriage rolled forward. Making an ever-widening circle around the market district, Seth searched as Maeve had asked. We passed many homes and businesses, most shuttered and dark. There were no children running through the streets or hiding in the shadows in any of the roads we traversed. At one common well, several women wore shawls over their mouths as they collected water. It was hard not to worry when faced with so much quiet despair.

Finally, the carriage slowed. Porcia leaned to look out the window with me.

"Madame Blye's Exquisite Trousseau and Accoutrement," Porcia said. "At least it's a well-known establishment. I was worried we'd end up at the docks looking for someone to sew."

"Nonsense," Maeve said. "I would never allow such a thing. Let's go in, my dears."

I waited, exiting the carriage last. Seth's hand closed around mine as he helped me down, and the warm way his fingers caressed my skin as he released me sent a coil of disgust straight to my stomach.

"Wait with the carriage," Maeve said. "We won't be long."

The bell above the door rang as Cecilia entered first. At the sound, a woman, dressed in a gown far too grand for a seamstress, straightened from her task of folding cloth samples.

"Good afternoon," she greeted us with a smile. "I'm Madame Blye. How may I help you?"

"We require gowns for the ball in two days' time," Maeve said. "Can you accommodate us?"

The woman's gaze swept over us. "Four gowns in two days?" She turned her head and lightly coughed into a white linen cloth she still held.

"Only two," Maeve said. "If you're too ill, I can—"

"Think nothing of my cough," the woman said. "I would be honored to create two exquisite gowns for you. Let's take some measurements and look at the cloth I have to offer, shall we? Then, we can discuss costs."

While Porcia and Cecilia stood for measurements, Maeve wandered the shop, looking at the various samples of cloth. I followed her, unable to endure more than ten feet between us before I felt the sickening pull to return to her side.

"What do you think of this color for Cecilia?" Maeve asked, holding up a lavender swatch. I considered it.

"It seems too subtle a color for Cecilia. What she wears should demand the attention she wants, should it not?"

Maeve sighed.

"You disappoint me."

My brows rose in surprise. "You truly want her to blend with all the other young women who will be there?"

"Not that." Maeve moved farther away from the

seamstress as the woman discussed skirt sizes and embellishments with Cecilia and Porcia. Between the conversation and her coughing, I knew she wasn't listening to my discussion with Maeve.

"You are correct that the lavender will not do," Maeve said. "My disappointment is in your choice to spurn your gifts of beauty and intelligence when it should be you standing for a fitting."

While she acted like she wanted me to be fitted as one of her obedient daughters, I knew she hadn't absolved me of the mirror's destruction or my lies of omission. So I said nothing, knowing no answer I gave would be suitable. Instead, I focused on the colors before me.

"Red would be too bold and matronly," I said. "What about this subtle rose color?"

Maeve nodded her approval, and I looked at Porcia before returning to the colors.

"Porcia's fair skin and dark hair will make this a sound choice for her." I touched a cloth that was a deeper shade of purple than the lavender but not so bold as to make her look matronly.

"Very well done," Maeve said. She took the two choices and gave them to Madame Blye just as she finished the last measurements.

"I'll deliver the dresses to the estate, myself, the day after tomorrow to make final adjustments," she said.

"Very good." Maeve handed over a purse heavy with

coin. "Ensure they are the best gowns to be seen at the ball, and we will return for more."

Based on the look on Madame Blye's face, the dresses would be as exquisite as her establishment's sign boasted.

"There's a cobbler, three doors down," she said. "If you stop there for measurements, I will ensure he has the material needed to make fine slippers to match."

Cecilia's eyes lit with delight, and Maeve nodded her agreement.

The cobbler greeted us as warmly as Madame Blye had and with the same cough. He promised to deliver the shoes to the seamstress so Cecilia and Porcia would have everything they needed to make a grand impression at the ball.

Giddy with excitement, the pair left the shop. I resented their behavior. This wasn't just an idle girl's fancy to go to the ball at the palace. This was so much more. It was a step in the right direction for them to achieve their goals. Despite Maeve's words that it should have been me preparing for the ball, I was relieved I was not. Free of the fittings and other obligations, I would have the time to plot and discover a way to put an end to Maeve's plans for good.

The desolation of the street outside the cobbler's cottage affirmed my need to do so quickly. Yes, the people of Towdown would recover when the bells chimed, but what about the next time Maeve sought to use them to force the King's hand? I'd witnessed the depths of her evil and feared for the kingdom's future if she succeeded.

In the carriage, I leaned against the seat, more than ready to return to the estate. However, the carriage did not head northwest as I expected.

"Where are we going?" I asked.

"To find the caster helping you, of course."

My stomach pitched violently, and I struggled to keep the fear from my eyes. Instead, I turned to look out the window. I watched the passing homes until I realized our direction. The Brazen Belle. How could she know? Had she witnessed it in the mirror?

As if reading my mind, Maeve began to speak.

"While traveling, I gave your problem great thought. The spell of protection woven into your being would have required a caster of great power and knowledge. It's an ability I would have sensed if it had been near me. While it is possible the caster could have come to the estate while I was away, there was another opportune moment that stood out to me. One instance where you were missing, and I was unable to locate you with the mirror."

She smiled and smoothed a hand over my hair.

"When I find your acquaintance at the Brazen Belle, we will put an end to the nasty spells keeping you from learning your lessons as a proper young lady should."

I couldn't speak. Fear closed my throat. I'd thought I'd been so clever with my excuse, but Maeve had still seen my absence for what it had been.

Through my ignorance and arrogance, I'd killed Rose.

The carriage came to a stop, and I looked out the

window at the Brazen Belle. Women stood on the porch. Their overflowing bosoms made their purpose clear. However, there were no merry calls this time, only coughing and idle stares at our carriage.

In the shade on the far side of the porch, Rose sat in her chair. She looked up and met my gaze briefly before returning to shelling her peas. She too coughed lightly, her cloth coming away bloody.

Maeve pulled me back from the window.

"It is best not to be seen here, my dear," she said, her eyes narrowing as she stared blankly in Porcia and Cecilia's direction.

"I sense no one of strength," Maeve said. "But if she's as strong as I believe, perhaps she's masking her presence as I've been masking mine." Maeve reached into her bodice and withdrew a vial which she handed to Cecilia.

"Go inside and speak with the others. Find out who has been casting and why. See if any recall Eloise's visit. And ask if there are any who are not ill."

Cecilia nodded, drank the vial, and left the carriage as a brunette marked with pox.

"Do you think anyone remembers dresses?" I asked, idly.

Maeve considered me for a moment.

"A very valid observation. I will tell Cecilia not to wear that dress in public again."

I cursed myself for saying anything.

We waited in the carriage for a long while before Cecilia returned.

"There are no new casters at the Brazen Belle. Those there still hold true to the oath they gave, verified by their blood."

"Freely given?" Maeve asked.

"Yes. All of them."

Maeve frowned, and her calculating gaze pinned me.

"Your choices are making things more difficult than they need to be."

She rapped on the carriage, and it started forward. Relief swam through my veins, and I resisted the urge to look out the window at Rose. Was she as powerful as Maeve suggested? I hoped so. For she might be the answer to stopping Maeve. Bound as I was to the estate, how would I ever get to her alone again, though?

Maeve interrupted my thoughts with thoughts of her own.

"We need to ensure this other caster will not interfere. We're too close now. There's no choice but to cast a location spell."

Cecilia and Porcia nodded, but I noticed the sudden sickly pallor in Porcia's face. Any relief I felt died. What did Maeve plan to do that had Porcia reacting so?

Maeve waited until the carriage was on the outskirts to knock on the top. As it slowed to a stop, she handed Porcia a purse heavy with coin.

"Be quick about it."

Cecilia nodded and grabbed her sister's hand. I watched out the window as they knocked on the door of a cottage. A thin woman answered. It was apparent she'd been ill long before Maeve's spell.

Maeve rapped on the roof again, and with a cluck from Seth, the carriage lurched forward.

"We aren't waiting for them?"

"No. People will note a carriage that lingers."

We drove a fair distance before Maeve stopped our progress once again. There, we waited. When Cecilia opened the door, her smile was wide.

"Fate was with us, Mama," she handed the coin purse back to Maeve. "The woman was amiable, and the child barely two."

"Well done."

Confused, I looked at Porcia. The girl's face was completely washed of any color.

"Are you well, Porcia?" I asked.

"Yes," she said woodenly. "Quite well, sister."

Maeve smiled.

"I know it wasn't easy on you, dear one. But remember, the younger the child..."

"The more powerful the magic," Porcia said, her hands tightly clasped in her lap. It was then I noticed the blood on them.

Maeve tapped on the roof to start the carriage moving.

"Let's hurry home before the heart cools. The magic is

stronger when fresh," she said, examining the dark coin purse that glistened wetly.

Horror consumed me, and Cecilia chuckled softly, witnessing it.

"You said no one would die." My words grew rough with anger and sorrow.

"I said no maids would die," Maeve replied. "Did you honestly believe I would let your act of defiance go without consequence? I will find the person helping you and destroy her. No one will stand in my way."

CHAPTER THREE

I SAT ON JUDITH'S OLD BED AND RAN MY HANDS OVER THE sheets. The image of a small heart in a bowl filled with bloody water kept swimming before my eyes, no matter how hard I tried not to see it. The detachment I'd thought I'd gained was a lie. Shivering, I wrapped my arms around myself and let the tears fall.

Thoughts of the child whose life had been stolen consumed me and filled me with impotent rage. I wanted to scream and hurt everyone around me. I wanted to make them feel the pain I felt. Feel the pain of their victims.

These feelings had consumed me the moment I'd understood what was in the bag. So much so that I'd almost struck out at Maeve during the spell. The very knife she'd used to drain the tiny heart of its remaining blood had been right there on the butcher block.

It was only the thought of the consequences if I failed

that had stayed my hand. I might hurt Maeve with a knife, but would I kill her? It wasn't a question of conviction—for I was more than willing to end her life—but a matter of strength and power. I overcame Hugh because he had wanted his end. But what of someone who didn't? In addition to her determination, Maeve had untold power. What if she had a spell protecting her as I had protecting me?

No, I couldn't let my temper rule me. I needed to think. To be detached. Yet, how could I after what I'd witnessed?

A scuff of noise came from the kitchen. I wiped away my tears, the only evidence of my momentary frailty, and stood just as Porcia appeared in the doorway.

Her face had regained a bit of her color since returning home.

"Mama is indisposed. There's no need to prepare a meal tonight."

I nodded, but she didn't leave. She stared at me for a moment then looked behind her before stepping into the room and closing the door.

"Things have been bad for you. But they can become much worse. Consider every consequence before you act. Please." She turned, reaching for the door. "For all our sakes."

She left, and I sat, thinking again of the heart in the bowl.

Much to Maeve's extreme displeasure, the spell hadn't worked. The child had died in vain, for the spell had shown nothing but mist when asked for the location of my co-conspirator. I doubted such a small victory could have felt emptier.

THE COCK'S crow woke me, and for a moment, my mind clung to the past. I rose from bed, thinking I would quietly sneak from the room so as to not wake Kellen on my way to feed the animals. But, the room wasn't my own. I looked down at Judith's bed and felt that tiny spark of joy I'd once felt rising at dawn fade into nothing.

Kellen was gone, hidden in the Dark Forest, afflicted by some unknown spell hidden in an apple. Father was missing, and Mother dead along with Anne and Judith and so many others. My will to carry on vanished. Why did one kingdom's fate matter so much? I thought of my playful talks with Kellen about leaving and traveling to see new lands. Why couldn't I do that? My chest squeezed as I recalled the spell trapping me here. There was no choice but to carry on.

Leaving the house, I fed the animals, promising the pig a walk soon before returning to the kitchen to start breakfast. I kept it to a simple meal of hot oats, toasted like Heather and Catherine had taught me.

When Maeve came down, I had the three bowls set on the table.

"You are missing a setting," she said. "Fetch your bowl."

I went back to the kitchen to serve myself a second portion, since I had already eaten. When I returned, Cecilia and Porcia were at the table. I sat to Maeve's right and waited for her to take the first bite.

"Very good," she said. "If only you were as useful a daughter as you are a maid."

I remained quiet and endured Cecilia's smirk as I ate.

From outside, a faint clanging reached my ears, and I paused with the spoon partway to my mouth. Maeve tilted her head, listening as well. A slow smile parted Maeve's lips at the distant sound of bells.

"Our divine prince has finally returned," she said. "I knew he wouldn't disappoint. Eloise, please tell Seth we will need him to go to market for us today. We're low on supplies." She looked at Porcia. "You can accompany him."

"Yes, Mama," Porcia and I said at almost the same time.

I ate quickly and went to the kitchen with my bowl. There, I hesitated. Maeve's command not to prepare a dinner the night before had meant the household went hungry. Unwilling to act heartlessly toward the man when he'd done nothing to deserve such treatment, I refilled my bowl for him and carried it outside.

I hadn't seen Seth since we'd returned from town but knew he'd made himself at home in Hugh's old room. I approached with a healthy amount of trepidation that had nothing to do with Seth and everything to do with the memories of the friend I'd lost.

Knocking on his door, I waited.

"Enter," Seth called.

I walked in and almost dropped the bowl. Completely naked and uncovered, Seth lay on his bed. He smiled at my shocked expression and reached down to grab himself.

"I'd rather hoped it would be you she sent to me."

"Mama said you will need to go to the market today for supplies." I set the bowl on his stove, not caring if it was hot or if it would ruin the dish. "Porcia will be going with you."

I turned and rushed out the door. He swore behind me, and I knew he would give chase. I picked up my skirts and ran with everything I had back to the house. When I flew into the kitchen, Porcia was there with the bowls from the dining room and looked up at me in astonishment.

"What is it?" she asked.

"Seth," I gasped.

She glanced behind me and frowned. I looked and saw an empty yard. Closing the door with shaky hands, I faced her.

"I believe he thought I was there to..."

"Fuck?"

I cringed at the use of the word but nodded.

"We must tell Mama. She was very clear to him."

She saw the apprehension in my eyes.

"It is better to tell her now than to be caught in a position where it might look like you're trying to steal her favorite toy."

She took my hand and led me to the dining room where Maeve still sat sipping tea.

"Mama," Porcia said. "Eloise had some trouble with Seth."

Her cool gaze shifted to me.

"Oh?"

"He was lying on the bed. Naked. Touching himself," I said.

She smiled slightly.

"I would have thought after your time in the Brazen Belle, something like that wouldn't be so shocking."

"He said he had hoped it was me you would send."

Her humor faded.

"I see. And did you hope I would send you to him?"

I shook my head vehemently.

"Good. I will not have you soiling yourself on someone such as him. You and your sister have more value if you are pure."

My gaze shifted to Porcia before I could stop myself.

"Speak," Maeve said.

"But didn't you tell Cecilia to measure Seth's worth before bringing him home?" I asked, using her own words.

Maeve waved away my concern.

"Cecilia lost her virginity long ago. You and Porcia are my pure ones." She rose and smiled at me. "That purity will be put to good use, have no doubt."

I waited until she left the room to look at Porcia.

"What does she mean?"

"After Cecilia passes the tests and weds the Prince, one

of us will need to take her place to consummate the marriage. I'm glad you look more like Cecilia."

SWEAT AND DUST coated my skin as I dragged the heavy piece of furniture across the floor. Before Cecilia's destructive rage, I hadn't realized how much the dust covers were hiding. The amount of furniture in the attic was maddening. Unwilling to stack it again—any walls I made would likely fall based on Cecilia's whims—I tried to sensibly place what was there.

I had several sitting areas, four sleeping areas, and a line of washbasins in addition to trunks and armoires tucked into every corner possible. The space was cluttered but still passable.

"Eloise," Porcia called. "The seamstress is here. You're needed."

After telling me yesterday that I would be the virgin sacrifice on the Prince's wedding night, everyone had left me alone. Oh, I'd ensured the meals were made and waited table, but instead of joining them, I worked in my attic space, desperate for solitude so I could think. Unfortunately, nothing had sparked any inspiring ideas to free me and end Maeve's madness.

Wiping back the hair stuck to my forehead, I descended from my space. In the sitting room, I found the seamstress already unpacking a large trunk. Gone was her pallor and cough. Yesterday's bells had indeed broken the curse.

The seamstress saw me and waved me forward.

"Finish unpacking the second dress. Lay it out, and smooth away what wrinkles you can. After I finish with them, they'll need to be hung until tonight. I'll show you how to lace them up."

Cecilia, already standing on the hemming stool in the center of the open space, snickered. I glanced at Maeve, and she nodded.

Doing as Madame Blye dictated, I started pulling the dress from the trunk.

"Be careful," she said harshly. "The lace is delicate and will rip."

Taking more care, I worked in silence and wondered what new twist this was in Maeve's game. She said I was a daughter and that I should eat at the table. She valued appearances above all else. A thought struck me, and I frowned as I smoothed out any wrinkles I spotted in the overabundance of lace on Porcia's gown. If Maeve was allowing this lesser known seamstress to treat me like a servant, it meant my appearance as a respectable young woman no longer mattered. Once I performed my task as a sacrifice, I wouldn't be needed.

I took a fortifying breath and laid the gown over Mother's settee. Being aware of my definitive end wasn't a bad thing. I now knew how much time I had to stop Maeve.

Right up until the wedding night...if I couldn't stop the wedding from happening in the first place.

"Girl," Madame Blye called. "Come here and hold this."

Accepting the pin cushion, I silently stood beside Cecilia as the seamstress knelt at her feet and praised my stepsister from her shiny hair to her beautifully long and narrow feet.

"You will adore the slippers the cobbler prepared for you. I managed to procure glass beads that will perfectly match the dress. When the toe of your slipper peeks from the hem, the glass will catch the light and sparkle beautifully."

The seamstress glanced at me.

"Get the shoes."

I didn't care for the woman. The way she fawned over Maeve, Cecilia, and Porcia then turned to me with a glint of disdain showed her true nature. Kindness was something that should be offered to all, not only those of wealth.

Turning to retrieve the shoes, I noted with a critical eye that the small band of beads sewn across the toe would hardly catch enough light to make them stand out. However, I kept the thought to myself as I offered the shoes to the woman.

"Help her put them on," she said, standing. She looked at Porcia. "Let's get you in your dress while they work."

I knelt at Cecilia's feet and held out one slipper.

"What do you think of my dress, Eloise?" Cecilia asked, lifting her foot.

I glanced up, taking measure of the seamstress's work. While the style was current and the color complementary, the embellishments were too numerous to let the color and design shine.

"You will stand out among the crowd and certainly draw the attention of the Royal family." I glanced at Porcia's gown, the skirt wider with its cascade of laced ruffles. "You both will."

Porcia smiled and looked to Maeve for approval.

"You're both lovely, my darlings."

Cecilia nudged me with the toe of her other foot, and I slid the second slipper on for her. When she stepped off of the stool, the skirt's back barely brushed the ground as she walked.

The seamstress made sounds of appreciation and helped Porcia onto the stool. We repeated the process for her, including the beaded slippers, then Madame Blye showed me how to lace and unlace the gowns as if I'd never worn such apparel myself. While mine hadn't ever been as grossly ornate, I had certainly worked lacings before.

I endured it all in silence and stood by as she packed up her stool into the small trunk.

"I hope you're pleased with the gowns," she said to Maeve.

"Indeed, I am."

"Would you like me to create two more for the next ball? I heard it is to occur this same day next week."

"Please. I would like final approval on color, however."

"Splendid. I will set aside some swatches for you." The seamstress turned to me. "Take the trunk to my wagon."

When I glanced at Maeve, she arched a brow at me. Not bothering to try to understand her purpose, I carried the trunk out. Once I was done loading it, I went to gather the pig for a walk. He squealed excitedly when he saw me.

After a jaunt in the trees between the cliff and Mother's clearing, I returned to the house and found the wagon gone.

"Eloise," Maeve called from the kitchen door. "Stop worrying about that pig. You need to heat bath water."

The pig squealed softly and ran for his enclosure as I quickly closed the gate.

"Hurry," she said as I crossed the yard. "We have much to do before dusk."

For the next several hours, I was in every sense of the word a lady's maid. I hauled water, helped my stepsisters wash their hair, brushed their hair until it shone beautifully, then helped them dress.

"Are you sure we should leave their hair down?" Maeve asked, studying her daughters with a critical eye.

"I only know how to braid hair," I said with an insincere apologetic shrug.

Maeve waved Cecilia forward and twisted her hair into a coil. Pinning that to Cecilia's head, Maeve let the end cascade down over Cecilia's shoulder.

"Porcia, yours will have to do. We're out of time."

I looked at the window and saw she was right. Dusk had fallen.

"Cecilia. Porcia. I will meet you in the carriage."

Cecilia smirked as she strode past me. Did she truly believe I cared that she was going to a ball and I wasn't?

"Eloise," Maeve said, drawing my attention. "There is laundry to be done and our rooms need to be straightened. If that's not enough to keep you occupied while we're gone, you can also clean out the pig's pen. There will be no more defiance. Do you understand?"

"Yes, Mama."

She nodded and hugged me as if her threat was an idle one, but we both knew differently. I watched her sweep from the room and slowly followed to listen for the sound of the carriage leaving. When it did, I raced upstairs to finish everything she said. I didn't care about impressing her; I wanted to finish quickly so I could go to the tree.

It took me over an hour before I had the wash hung outside and turned to the pig's pen. The task was certainly meant as a form of punishment, but I truly didn't mind it. However, by the time I finished, my back was sore, and I reeked fiercely.

"I wish I could bathe in the pond," I said to the pig as I closed the gate. He squealed and trotted toward me as if he thought it was a good idea.

"Like you, I'm stuck here. Swimming will have to wait." I threw him a wilted carrot, which I'd stuck in my pocket, and turned toward the path leading to Mother's clearing.

The night was quiet and the light breeze welcome as I sat under the stars. In the branches of the tree, the bird chirped to me softly before hushing once more.

"I've gotten myself in quite a tangle this time," I said softly. "If you're listening, I need help. Desperately. If there's a way to stop the Prince from marrying anyone at that ball tonight, please...tell me. Show me a sign. Give me something." I sighed and closed my eyes, tilting my head to the night sky.

The bird chirped. Once. Twice. Then it broke out into a merry song meant for the bright light of the rising sun. I opened my eyes, scanning the tree, and gasped at the twinkling bit of moonlit silver in the branches. As I watched, the bird pushed the object from the branch on which it rested and it fluttered to the ground. I rose, approaching cautiously.

The bird silenced as I reached the fallen mask. Picking it up, I marveled at the ornate work. Silver threads attached flakes of thin silver to the edge of the mask. Chips of clear stone inlaid in a cord of silk just inside that, then more silver embroidery imbedded the pale blue cloth that made up the mask. The silken ribbons teased my dirty fingers but did not become dirty. Truly, the mask was a gift made by magic. But to what purpose?

I looked up at the bird.

"I don't understand."

It chirped at me then tucked its beak under its wing.

Frowning, I tied the mask to my face. The world looked

no different through it. But perhaps wearing a mask would trick Maeve's spell into thinking I could leave? I had no other guess why the bird would give me such a thing.

Hurrying through the woods, I entered the yard and strode down the driveway. As soon as I reached the same spot as the day before, I went flying backwards and landed hard on my backside.

"That wasn't supposed to happen," I mumbled, picking myself up slowly. Frustrated, I went to the well to wash then returned to my attic space where I hid the mask behind the chimney.

"What good is a mask when I can't leave the estate?" I grumbled. As much as I wanted to return to the tree and try again, I didn't dare. If Maeve felt me try to leave, she would undoubtedly return soon. It was better to let her find me sleeping.

Laying down, I closed my eyes.

It felt like only moments later that I was rudely pushed.

"Get up. This instant."

I registered the anger in Maeve's voice and quickly obeyed, getting to my feet before my eyes fully opened.

"Who was it?" she demanded.

"Huh?" I didn't mean to let my ineloquent confusion slip, but my mind was still slumbering peacefully.

"Who came to you?"

I blinked at her and frowned. She grabbed my throat, and I felt the warm tingle of a spell.

"Speak," she commanded.

"No one came here. I straightened the rooms, did the laundry, cleaned the pig's pen, and went to bed. My only company was the pig and a bird," I said.

She pushed me to my bed, and I winced at the contact. She noticed and narrowed her eyes at me.

"How are you hurt?"

"Not hurt. Sore from my labors."

Her anger melted away.

"Porcia, check the pig's pen. Tell me if it's properly cleaned." She glanced at Cecilia. "Check the laundry." Cecilia gave me an evil grin and left the attic.

"We both know she's going to dirty what I already washed and claim it wasn't done correctly."

Maeve smiled slightly.

"Then you had better get up from your bed if you want any sleep tonight. Henceforth, I expect you to be by the door, waiting for us when we arrive home."

Maeve turned to leave.

"And wash your dress. I won't tolerate that smell in my home."

CHAPTER FOUR

TIREDLY, I CLEANED THE BREAKFAST DISHES. AFTER rewashing all of the clothing that Cecilia had stomped into the dirt, I'd managed to return to my bed only an hour before dawn. However, I'd known I would need to rise with the cockcrow, regardless.

"We need to find out who that fat cow in the yellow dress was," Cecilia said. "She had the nerve to cut in front of me in line."

"I'm surprised you allowed it," Porcia said.

"If there had been a discreet way to remove her, I would have. The Prince would have noticed, though. Better to look kind than vengeful."

"Very true, sister."

While Maeve was still abed, Cecilia and Porcia were awake and at the kitchen table. I wished they would just leave. I'd fed them. Why stay?

"He was ever so handsome, don't you agree, Porcia?"

I rolled my eyes at Cecilia's obvious attempt to make me feel jealous.

"So very handsome," Porcia agreed. "I nearly fainted when he placed his hand on my waist. You're ever so lucky you managed a second dance."

"Luck had nothing to do with it. We spoke during our first dance. Of nothing important really, but he seemed pleased with me enough to seek me out again."

Her fingers thrummed over the wood planks.

"Did you note the lump of his amulet hidden by his cravat?" Cecilia asked.

"No. How did you?"

Cecilia chuckled.

"A well-timed collision with another couple. He was ever so apologetic about it. The incident has me wondering if it might be possible to damage it during the next ball."

"Possibly," Porcia said. "Even the smallest fracture would weaken the amulet. If it were discovered, though, would that possibly jeopardize the next ball?"

"Perhaps. We will need to discuss this opportunity with Mama."

Behind me, the bench scraped against the floor, and I felt a small measure of relief that they were leaving. Once they did, I planned to go back to bed.

"You've been quiet this morning, dear sister," Cecilia said. "Staying here when we went to the ball must have been difficult. If you ask me nicely, I will speak on your behalf to Mama."

I glanced back at Cecilia.

"The only purpose for attending the ball is to win the Prince. Do you truly want me to compete against you, Cecilia?"

"Do you truly believe you could win?" she asked, her eyes narrowing at me. "The mirror might be able to see beyond your filth, but I doubt the prince will. He's led a life of privilege, and that has blinded better men than this kingdom's princeling. He will see you as nothing more than the worthless girl you are."

"Who are you trying to convince? Me or yourself?"

Cecilia pivoted and stormed from the room. Porcia let an exasperated sigh slip.

"You truly have no sense."

A clatter arose outside, and for a moment, I wondered what Cecilia was doing. Then, hounds started to bark. Porcia and I made for the door at the same time. When we stepped outside, the dust from wagons and horses passing on the road to the Retreat drifted on the air and made us cough.

A rider emerged, trotting up our drive. He wore the same attire as Kaven.

"Ho, Cartwright family," the man called cheerily.

Porcia and I shared a glance just before he pulled to a stop before us.

"The Prince has returned and is taking up residence at the

Royal Retreat. He humbly asks that you stay on the land allotted to you as he plans to hunt the woods while here. If you have any questions or concerns, please send your man to the Retreat." He tipped his hat to us and wheeled his horse around to return to the caravan still proceeding to the Retreat.

"Mama will be so pleased," Porcia said neutrally. "I'd best tell her."

I turned to follow her into the house and wished the Prince was there so I might strangle him. How much had I lost, all in Maeve's pursuit of the Prince? And here he was, coming to live right next to them. I debated if the man was really worth saving. He'd been an ass when questioning me in the dungeon. Perhaps Cecilia was right, and a life of privilege had made him blind. However, a blind king was better than a vindictive, power-hungry queen.

Cecilia's squeal of delight rang through the house just as I stepped inside. I hoped this news would be enough to keep her from wrecking my room again.

Groaning, I sank deeper into the tub of hot water. The dining room door swung open, and Cecilia strode in.

"What do you think you're doing?" she demanded.

I dipped my head under the water, ignoring her, only to be yanked up by my hair a moment later. Her face was contorted with anger as she tugged harder.

"You do realize that doesn't hurt, don't you?"

She growled and shoved me under.

Instead of fighting her, I used my hands to douse her in as much water as I could. She released me and stepped back just as Maeve entered.

"What is the noise in here?" she asked.

"Cecilia was trying to drown me," I said before Cecilia could think of anything to explain her waterlogged state.

"I will not tolerate any more disturbances. Not while the Prince is in residence. Do you understand, Cecilia? Keep your jealousy to yourself, or it might be observed at the most inopportune time."

"Yes, Mama," she said between clenched teeth.

"Is there a reason you came in here?"

Cecilia remained mute. However, I knew the only reason was to torment me because she hadn't forgotten my remark from this morning.

"Go," Maeve said. "Leave Eloise alone. I will not warn you again."

"Yes, Mama."

Cecilia left me with Maeve. The woman considered me for a moment then sat on the stool near the tub.

"Thank you for bathing," she said. "I almost couldn't eat dinner."

After hearing the news of the Prince's arrival, Maeve had ordered the house cleaned from top to bottom. I'd spent hours doing as she'd bid. So many that I hadn't had to step foot in the kitchen, much to Porcia's dismay. So many that my body ached each time I moved.

Maeve continued to study me, making me wish the bathwater wasn't so clear.

"Did you need me to do something else?" I risked asking.

"Not tonight. You did well today. Dare I hope you've learned your lesson?" she asked.

I couldn't even recall why I was being punished anymore. Then I remembered the mirror.

"I shouldn't have tried to damage what was yours," I said. "I know that now."

She made a noncommittal noise.

"Come to me if your sister causes trouble," she said, rising. "The remainder of this day is yours to do with as you choose. So long as you stay on the estate."

She left the room, and I sagged against the edge of the tub. The only thing I wanted to do was sleep. However, the thump of furniture from above had me revising my plans for the evening. After washing away the lingering odor from cleaning the pig's pen from my hair, I dried, dressed, and slipped out the door.

Movement across the yard had me looking at the shed, where Seth leaned against its wall. His gaze swept over me, but he remained where he was. I debated going back inside then strode toward the path to Mother's clearing. I'd used a rock to bash one man upside the head and a chain to kill another. I wasn't helpless, and I refused to live in fear of Seth. There were far too many things I feared already.

In the fading light of the clearing, I sat on the bench with a sigh. For several minutes, I remained silent in an attempt to absorb the tranquility of the place. Too many thoughts crowded my mind to find peace, however.

I looked at the bird watching me from its perch, not joining the chorus of the other creatures around us.

"There's so much I want to tell you," I said. "I wish—"

A branch snapped, and I looked over to find Kaven on the other side of the clearing.

"Please don't stop. I didn't mean to intrude." He turned as if to leave. As much as I knew I should let him go, I was desperate for his company.

"It's okay. There's nothing I can say anyway."

He hesitated, studying me.

"Why not?"

I smiled slightly.

"Is this an attempt to persuade me to reveal my innermost secrets to you?"

He chuckled and crossed the clearing to sit beside me.

"I've missed you," he said.

As soon as he said the words, I realized how much I'd missed him, too. Knowing he'd been at the Retreat had been a comfort.

"And I you," I said softly. I studied him for a moment. "I was worried."

"You were? Why?"

"The last time I saw you, you were coughing like so many others."

Something flashed in his eyes before he looked away.

"What?" I asked.

He reached for my hand, lacing his fingers through mine. His warm touch sent a shiver through me. His eyes darkened, and his gaze dipped to my mouth briefly.

"I shouldn't have kissed you. It was a foolish, selfish thing to do." He caught my frown and smiled slightly. "Don't mistake me. I would kiss you again if you would allow me. But to kiss you when I was ill...I risked you."

I didn't know what to say because I'd never been at risk.

"The past cannot be undone," I said softly. "That is a truth with which I've come to terms. Don't let regret rob you of the here and now because I don't regret our kiss either."

He released my hand to gently run his fingers along my jaw.

"Eloise, I've grown far too fond of you," he said. "I can think of little else but your sharp tongue, mocking gaze, or sweet lips."

"That hardly sounds complimentary."

"Oh, it is. You've captured my interest like no other because you are like no other. I enjoy your wit and your charm when you choose to use them. Tell me there will be a day when you will be mine."

I frowned slightly.

"What exactly are you asking?"

He glanced down at my lips again and chuckled softly.

"Nothing I have the right to ask of you. Yet."

Before I could guess his intent, his fingers delved into my hair and his lips met mine. My heart gave a jolt before warmth spread like fire through my body. His tongue teased the seam of my mouth, and I gasped. With a groan, he swept inside. The first touch of his tongue to mine robbed me of all thought. I didn't know how long I lost myself to the feel of him before I heard a throat clearing.

Pushing away from him, I glanced at Kaven with wide eyes before looking at Cecilia, who stood on the path.

"My," she said fanning herself. "When Mama sent me to fetch you, I wasn't expecting to find this."

Panic rising, I stood.

"This isn't what it looks like," I said.

"I'm sure it's not," Cecilia said agreeably before looking at Kaven. "And who might you be?"

She knew very well who he was after witnessing my prior attempts to seduce him.

"This is Kaven," I said quickly. "He's here with the Prince."

"Ah. One of the Prince's servants."

Kaven gave her a deep bow.

"At your service, miss...?"

"Cecilia. I'm Eloise's sister."

"It's a pleasure to make your acquaintance. Please let your mother know I will call upon the Cartwright house tomorrow."

Cecilia's smile widened.

"I most certainly will. Come, Eloise. We had better return. Mama is expecting us."

I glanced at Kaven, wishing I could warn him in some way, but there was nothing I could say. Especially not in front of Cecilia.

Without a word, I turned from him and hurried toward the path, ignoring Cecilia's knowing smirk. She followed me, keeping pace until we reached the yard then she lifted her skirts to hurry to the house. Knowing her intent, I did not let her outpace me. She laughed all the way to the sitting room.

"Mama," she said breathlessly, "Eloise has something to tell you."

Maeve looked up from the book she was reading.

"What is it?" she asked as she looked at me.

"Kaven kissed me," I said bluntly.

"And it looked like you were kissing him back," Cecilia added snidely.

I shrugged helplessly at Maeve.

"What else was I to do?"

"Slap him," Maeve said firmly, closing her book.

"But I thought we wanted him to—"

"You were to flirt with him, not encourage him." She tapped her fingers on the arm of her chair.

I looked at Cecilia then Maeve and let my frustration show.

"How am I supposed to know the difference? You

taught me how to flirt with him at a whorehouse. Everything that happened there was for encouragement. And certainly nothing showed me how to unflirt once I started."

Maeve stared at me for a moment then burst out laughing.

"Oh, Eloise. You are a treasure in your innocence. Even Porcia isn't so naïve."

I stood there, enduring her amusement. When she sobered, she stood and crossed the room to give my arm a reassuring squeeze.

"You made the best choice available to you. Don't worry about young Kaven. I will address the issue."

My stomach clenched with fear.

"You will have your chance tomorrow," Cecilia said. "He plans to call on us. See, sister? There's no need to worry."

I wanted to claw her eyes out.

THE KNOCK on the kitchen door paused my labor. I looked at Cecilia, who had been an annoyingly constant presence since the moment I woke. She rose from her spot at the table, took a pinch of flour to wipe on her cheek, and went to open the door.

"Good morning, Kaven," she said, pulling the door wider. "Do come in. Eloise and I were just baking bread."

My heart ached at the sight of him as he stepped into

the kitchen. As much as I feared for his safety and wished him away, I was also glad for his presence. His eyes swept the room, noting me before turning to Cecilia.

"You make your own bread?" he asked.

"It's much more cost effective than buying it at the market," she said, closing the door behind him.

He glanced at me, warmth lighting his eyes.

"It's not that. I thought ladies such as yourselves didn't need to bake."

"It's a skill that Mama insists every woman should master," Cecilia said. She gave Kaven a knowing smile. "I'm to fetch Mama. I'll be a few minutes."

He gave her a wide smile and a small bow.

"You have my gratitude."

As soon as the door closed he stepped toward me. My pulse raced with the understanding of his intent, and I held up both hands to stave him off.

"Don't," I warned.

He chuckled as if I played some cute game and caught me up in his arms. The press of his strong arms so firmly around my waist warmed my insides to a degree.

"But I've missed you," he said softly.

My heart gave an agreeable lurch at his sentiment. His blue gaze held mine expectantly, likely waiting for me to return his affection.

"Well, I haven't missed you," I lied. "Let me go before she returns."

I set my floured hands on his shoulders and pushed. He

didn't budge. Instead, he dipped his head and nuzzled my neck, sending tingles of awareness into places I shouldn't acknowledge. They were so delicious, however, that I gasped and stilled.

He groaned and nibbled the tender skin just below my ear.

"She said we have a few minutes," he said softly.

Realizing I'd weakened, I pushed at him again.

"She was lying."

As soon as the words were out of my mouth, the door opened.

"Release my daughter at once," Maeve said sternly but without anger.

Kaven did as he was told and bowed deeply to Maeve.

"I beg for your forgiveness and a private word with you, mistress."

"You are not forgiven, and you can speak your piece here," she said, unmoved by Kaven's attempt at a charming smile.

"I've come to speak my intentions for Eloise," he said formally.

"Your intentions? I see." Maeve's tone and expression gave nothing away. She appeared neither upset nor startled by the news as she glanced at me.

"Eloise has captured my heart," he said. "I'm here to ask—"

"I'm afraid such a match would be unsuitable," Maeve said, not unkindly. "Despite her current mode of dress, I would see her settled comfortably in life. And I believe you could not hope to give that to her as she has no dowry. This home belongs to the Crown as do most of the items within it. You have nothing to give her, and she has nothing for you. I'm sorry, Kaven, but my answer is no. Firmly, no."

I glanced at Kaven, my heart breaking. He didn't look at me but bowed again to Maeve.

"Thank you for hearing me. While I will respect your answer, please know that I also hope to change your mind."

"An impossibility," Maeve said. "It's time you leave."

"I see. With your permission, I have a message to deliver."

She nodded.

"Your family is invited to the Retreat this evening for dinner. The Prince has heard of Eloise and the stories regarding her mother. He's also interested in meeting the woman who now holds the title of Mistress Cartwright."

"Please let His Highness know that he honors us with his interest and invitation, and we humbly accept."

CHAPTER FIVE

"THIS WILL HAVE TO DO," MAEVE SAID, HOLDING UP ONE OF Cecilia's gowns to me.

That it was one she'd worn to the whorehouse didn't escape my notice. However, I doubted the Prince would know that.

"Porcia has more dresses than me, Mama. Perhaps we should try one of hers."

Maeve cut Cecilia a sharp look.

"You and Eloise share a similar shape, size, and coloring. She will wear one of your dresses, and you will say not a single word about it."

"Yes, Mama," she said softly.

"It's Eloise's interactions with that boy which have gained the attention of the Prince." Maeve focused on me, placing the dress in my arms. "Cecilia will accompany you on all your walks henceforth. Should you happen upon young Kaven, you will be chaperoned, and Cecilia will have an opportunity to impress him with her good nature as you have done."

"Yes, Mama," I said, cringing on the inside. I'd barely regained the small freedom of going outdoors, and now it was being taken from me yet again.

"Go dress. Make yourself presentable."

I turned to leave Cecilia's room, but Maeve stopped me with a question.

"Do you hold affection for the boy?" she asked.

"He is kind and handsome. I hold him in friendship, nothing more."

Maeve remained silent for a moment.

"Would you grieve his loss?"

Words escaped me as the pain of such an idea consumed me.

"I can see you would. Spare yourself such torment and behave accordingly tonight. Do you understand?"

"Yes, Mama." I cursed myself for showing even a hint of my affection for Kaven in front of her.

"Very good." She came to me and kissed my cheek. "Run along now. We will be waiting for you in the carriage."

I hurried upstairs to change. After a long day baking and cleaning, I would have preferred to crawl into my bed and sleep. However, I knew there would be no escaping the dinner to come. I resented the Prince's long overdue presence and hoped that tonight would proceed smoothly and spare Kaven any consequence of my folly.

Looking out at the moon shining through my small window, I thought of Kaven. My heart gave a lurch at the memory of his earnest offer for my hand. I let myself imagine a world where Maeve was stopped. A world where the King allowed Kaven and me to live here as man and wife. My skin flushed with the recollection of Kaven's kisses. Man and wife. For a moment, I let myself cling to that happy thought. I was tired of being so alone. And afraid. It was my fear that destroyed my dream. I couldn't allow my affection for Kaven to show. Until Maeve was stopped, I needed to keep him at a distance, no matter how much I wished to share the burden of my knowledge. I wouldn't condemn another to my hell.

As soon as I laced the dress and brushed out my hair, I went downstairs and found everyone already in the carriage. It seemed silly to have Seth drive us when the distance was so close, but Maeve was firm. Walking was for impoverished people who were beneath the Prince's notice.

I kept my thoughts of such ridiculousness to myself and watched out the window.

When we pulled into the yard, the door to the Retreat opened, and Kaven stepped out. I looked away quickly but not before I noted that he wore the same clothes from the morning. Or his welcoming smile at the sight of our carriage.

Seth opened the door for us, and Maeve descended first, followed by Cecilia, Porcia, and finally me.

"Welcome," Kaven said. "His Royal Highness is waiting for you in the parlor."

Kaven led the way to the room in question where the Prince struck a magnificent pose before the fire. His cropped dark brown hair was combed back in an overly perfect way that showcased his regal nose and cool blue-grey eyes. He breathed deeply as he watched us enter, the move expanding his chest and straining his jacket. It was a calculated move to impress his masculine presence upon us. I struggled not to snort and caught Kaven watching me. He winked, and I quickly looked away.

My gaze collided with the Prince's.

"Welcome to the Retreat," he said. "As we are neighbors, I thought it appropriate to make your acquaintance in person. Kaven spoke highly of you. Well, some of you."

I still hated the prick for my time in the dungeon and his condescending tone.

"Your Highness," Maeve said with a deep curtsy. "Allow me to introduce my daughters, Cecilia, Porcia, and Eloise."

While my sisters performed perfect curtsies, mine was half-hearted at best.

"Please rise," the Prince said. "Sit. Can I have my servant offer you anything to drink before we dine? I'm very interested to hear the story behind Mr. Cartwright's hasty marriage so soon after the infamous Mrs. Cartwright's demise."

My mouth dropped open. Could he be any ruder?

"Of course, Your Highness," Maeve said graciously. "Wine would benefit us all for such a tale."

He glanced at Kaven, who then left the room while Maeve sat near the Prince. Cecilia and Porcia hurried to take nearby seats as well. I kept my distance, choosing a chair as far as I could get from the Prince without making myself sick from the spell binding me to Maeve.

"What you must first know is that Atwell Cartwright loved Margaret without reservation, even in her slow deterioration. And, he saw their daughters as an extension of the remarkable woman he loved."

Maeve's words were making me ill, and it took everything in me not to let what I felt show in any way. One mistake a day was enough.

"He was as devoted to his children as I am to mine," she continued. "We both understood our children would be our future source of happiness. Thus, the day he received word of his wife's death, he came to me. As Margaret's cousin and a widow myself, he knew that I would be able to offer our children the protection they might need in his absence."

The Prince glanced at Cecilia and Porcia before his gaze landed on me. There was something in the depths of that look—a knowing, perhaps—that had me sitting straighter as he focused on Maeve again.

"And to where did Mr. Cartwright disappear? It seems odd he abandoned his children, you claim he loved well, so soon after losing his wife."

"Alas, his grief for his lost wife was greater than his love for the children they created."

Maeve's words echoed closely what I'd thought, myself. Yet, I hated her desperately for voicing such a lie, now, when we both knew it not to be true.

"He saw too much of Margaret in his children. I believe he sought to escape the reminder of what has now been lost to him."

"You do not seem upset by the news of your cousin's death," the Prince commented.

She shrugged slightly.

"I've suffered loss and know how the passing of time can dull the sharp edges of grief's pain. Atwell will learn that too, and if he is able, he will return."

"Why do you think he might not be able?"

"Before he left, he confided his plans to attempt to reestablish a trade route through the Dark Forest. Though I tried to dissuade him of the notion with a more suitable escape from pain, he was determined."

"Dare I ask what a more suitable escape would be?"

"Not in present company, Your Highness. While I'm a widow and well versed in what happens in a man's world, my daughters have been sheltered from such knowledge."

"Ah. I see."

His gaze once again swept over us before Kaven returned with flutes of wine.

"Thank you, Kaven."

"Of course, Your Highness. Dinner awaits your command."

Kaven served Maeve her drink first, leaving me for last. When he faced me, he smiled warmly and winked again. I tried to ignore him, but the wink made my heart race.

"Kaven has spoken highly of you, Eloise," the Prince said, calling my attention as Kaven left the room again. "I now feel the need to apologize to you for our first meeting."

Porcia choked on her drink and jerked her head toward me. Cecilia was subtler in her shock.

"First meeting, Your Highness?" Maeve asked.

Fear settled into the pit of my stomach.

"Eloise didn't tell you? I'm surprised. I would have thought she would have needed the comfort of a loved one after such a terrifying experience."

I could barely breathe. Though his concern and expression indicated genuine concern, the words were too provoking. It was almost as if he'd known I hadn't shared our meeting with Maeve. But, he couldn't possibly know the consequences of such a slip. Never had I been more grateful for the spell protecting me than at that moment. But what of Kaven?

Finding my voice, I grasped for the words that would salvage the situation.

"While I did indeed share my adventure in the dungeons with my family, I graciously omitted your involvement in hopes that you would make amends in person since we are neighbors. I didn't think an apology for dragging an innocent girl into your dungeon would take so long, though."

Silence reigned the room a moment before he laughed.

"I'm gladdened to see your time there did not dull the fire of your wit and sharp tongue." He strode toward me and offered his arm.

"Allow me to escort you to dinner to make up for my boorish behavior."

Having little choice, I stood and accepted. When he placed his hand over mine, I couldn't be sure whether it was due to him feeling my tremble of fear or just courtesy. We walked before the rest, leading the way to the dining room. I didn't note anything along the way. Instead, my fate when we returned home gripped my mind.

Kaven was there to pull out Maeve's chair as the Prince assisted me to mine. He was also the one who directed the rest of the staff to serve us.

The first course passed in relative silence. It gave me enough time to collect my thoughts and drive the conversation in a way that might just save Kaven from any harm.

"Did any maids catch your attention at the ball?" I asked bluntly.

"Eloise," Maeve said sharply.

The Prince chuckled.

"Do not let her direct nature concern you, mistress. My youth was filled with stories of her mother's similar directness. Therefore, I would expect no less from Eloise."

"You're too kind, Your Highness," Maeve said softly. I could hear the threat in her sweetness, though.

"What did you think of the ball?" he asked me.

"I prefer to keep my opinion of the balls to myself."

He laughed.

"It is far too late for you to withhold your thoughts now."

"Yes, Eloise," Maeve said. "Please, do entertain us with your thoughts."

"It seems silly to host balls where hundreds of women will vie for your attention when there are other means to get to know your prospective bride."

"Quite right," Cecilia said. "For example, intimate dinners such as this are much more conducive to conversation. Though I did so enjoy dancing with you at the first ball."

The Prince looked at Cecilia with a slightly puzzled frown.

"Perhaps Eloise is right about the balls being a fruitless endeavor. For my life, I cannot recall dancing with you. Although, I must admit my feet are still sore today from all the partners I twirled around the room."

Cecilia flushed slightly, her embarrassment, or perhaps anger, showing at his lack of recognition.

"You danced with me as well," Porcia said. "And I

sympathize with your plight. There were a great many ladies in attendance but so few men. It might behoove you to encourage more males to attend the next one so the line of maids waiting for your attention isn't so long."

"Are you suggesting that the maids attending would rather not catch my attention?"

Porcia flushed scarlet.

"I believe my sister was only offering a suggestion that might alleviate your woefully overused feet," I said. "However, it is also wise for you to recognize that not every maid might desire to wed a Prince."

The Prince glanced at me.

"Wise indeed," he murmured. "Tell me more of yourself, Eloise. What is it you like to do with your free time?"

"I'm quite dull, Your Majesty, and prefer to spend my idle time lost in a book."

"Or walking amongst the trees while listening to birds sing?" the Prince asked.

I glanced at Kaven, who stood off to the side of the room, near Maeve. He flashed me a quick smile, and I scowled before I could stop myself. His loose lips were going to cost us both dearly.

"While I grieve for my mother, yes, I walk among the trees," I said. "Cecilia, what do you most enjoy doing with your idle time since coming to the estate? And what do you miss most about your old home?"

She artfully kept the conversation centered on her

interests while the servants cleared our dishes for the next course. I inhaled the scent of perfectly cooked meat, and my mouth watered as my dish was set before me. A small, oblong loaf sat amidst a pool of gravy and roasted root vegetables.

"Cut into the bread," Kaven said, watching me.

Maeve glanced at me as well, a calculating look in her eye. Kaven needed to stop showing his interest in me.

"Kaven, why don't you help her?" the Prince suggested when I didn't move.

Kaven circled the table and leaned over me to cut my meat. I looked at the Prince with a smile.

"Thank you. It's a new dish for me. What is it called?"

"I haven't the faintest notion."

"Beef in a Blanket," Kaven said, close enough to my ear to send a shiver chasing down my spine. He placed my fork near my hand and stepped away.

"Kaven introduced me to this dish during our travels," the Prince said. "Not only is he usefully observant, he also has impeccable taste."

"That he does," Maeve said agreeably.

"How long has Kaven served you?" I asked.

The Prince glanced at Kaven, humor twinkling in his eyes.

"Since as long as I can remember. His father decided his fate at a young age, for which I'm very grateful. I couldn't imagine what would have become of me if not for Kaven's steadfast presence."

I looked at Kaven, too, and found him watching me, all humor absent from his gaze. Is that why he'd said he couldn't leave the Prince's service? Because Kaven was bound to the Prince for life? What good would my patience then do?

"It's very fortunate you have him, then," I said.

"Indeed. He has saved my life countless times. Poisoned food. Man-eating creatures set loose in my tent. There was even that time you—"

"Perhaps not an appropriate topic for the dining table," Kaven said softly.

"Too right," the Prince said with a smile before returning his attention to his food.

I took my first bite and tried to savor the food. However, I'd been with Maeve long enough to know the signs of her temper. Her quiet. Her rigid posture. Her very kind smile.

Through the remainder of the meal, Cecilia and Porcia both attempted to win the Prince's favor through conversation. Yet, it inevitably seemed to return to me.

"Would you walk with me, Eloise?" the Prince asked after we had finished eating.

I glanced at Maeve.

"I will allow it. With a chaperone, of course."

The Prince glanced at Porcia.

"You may follow us with Kaven's escort."

Porcia bowed her head and accepted Kaven's offered arm when he approached. I had no choice but to join the

Prince. My hand rested lightly on his sleeve as he led me from the dining room.

"Did you enjoy yourself this evening?" he asked.

"Yes, Your Majesty."

He directed us toward a trophy room adjoining the dining room. My stomach knotted uncomfortably with each step I took further away from Maeve. It was fortunate that I didn't go flying backward, though. Explaining that away would have been impossible, and I would have likely found myself back in the dungeon this evening, regardless of Kaven's fondness for me.

Rather than focus on my discomfort, I studied the stuffed remains of one of many creatures crowded throughout the entire space.

"What I want to show you is further in," the Prince said.

I continued onward, fighting the pull in my middle and the sickening need to return to Maeve.

"Here," he said, stopping.

I looked at the giant creature, surprise distracting me for a moment. Frozen in time, with its lips curled in a vicious snarl, the beast stood on two legs but was stooped. Wickedly sharp claws tipped every digit. Its head reminded me of both wolf and bear.

"What is it?" I asked.

"It's what your mother helped to stop. A creature made of magic and sickness. A creature that was once human."

"Human?" I said, looking closer.

"Yes. We aren't sure how it started, but we know how it

spread. With a bite, this creature would infect others. If not for your mother and her magic, the kingdom would have fallen."

I turned to the Prince. The hint of scornful patronization that had lingered in his tone since our first meeting was now absent, and I wasn't sure what that meant.

"You think my mother had magic?"

He smiled slightly.

"It would seem we were raised hearing different stories."

"I've heard none, actually. Not until after her passing."

"It saddened me to receive word that she had passed. I'm sorry for your loss. She did a great service for the kingdom." He took my hand and held it in his own as he looked at me.

I wasn't sure I cared for this new side of the Prince any more than I had the pompous side. I could no longer tell when a person was being true to their nature or hiding something more.

"You are one of the reasons I came to stay at the Retreat. I wanted to meet the Cartwright daughters. I'm curious where your sister is. Kellen, is it not?"

I eased my hand from his and stared at the beast once more.

"She left in the middle of the night to find our father," I said. "I can only hope that she's found him rather than beasts such as this when she entered the Dark Forest."

"She left? Alone? Why?"

"Why does anyone do anything rash?" I asked. "My stepmother sent men after her, but they haven't yet returned."

For a long moment, he said nothing.

"You've lost everyone you hold dear."

He had no idea how very much I had lost because of Maeve. A sudden pain knifed through my middle.

"Not everyone," I said with a smile I hardly felt. "I think we should perhaps return to the dining room."

He nodded and placed my hand on his arm. When his touch lingered, I moved my hand from under his.

"You don't care for me," he said.

"It's hard to care for someone I do not know."

"And equally hard to forgive mistreatment."

I looked up into his grey eyes.

"Very true, Your Majesty."

"I hope to sway your opinion of me."

We turned then, and I saw Porcia and Kaven only steps away. Porcia looked pale and flushed at the same time. Kaven looked annoyed. He looked pointedly at my hand on the Prince's arm. Really, what did Kaven expect me to do? Outright reject the Crowned Prince?

Ignoring him, I allowed the Prince to escort me back to the dining room.

"I look forward to seeing you soon," he said, releasing me. Then he honored me with a small bow.

"The Crown will forever be indebted to your family. As

soon as we are able, we will send men to look for your father and sister."

"Thank you," I said with a bow of my head, wishing instead I could kick the man. Why had he waited until we were in front of Maeve to say such a thing?

"We look forward to our next meeting," Maeve said as she and Cecilia joined us. We all gave our curtsies then departed.

The carriage had barely started forward when Maeve rounded on me. She hit me hard enough that my head twisted to the side, and my bones cracked. Thankfully, there was no pain.

"You knew? How dare you not tell me."

"Would it have changed your course?" I asked, looking at her. "He still needed to be flushed into the open. The spell would have still needed to be cast."

Her eyes narrowed.

"What else have you been keeping from me?"

"Nothing that you haven't already discovered."

She tilted her head, studying me.

"This sudden boldness is unwelcome. If you believe the Prince's momentary interest will protect you, you are wrong." She turned to Porcia. "What was said while they were alone?"

"He showed her the creatures that attacked the kingdom and said it was her mother's magic that saved everyone. Then, he said that she was the reason he came to the Retreat. To meet her and Kellen. When he asked where

Kellen was, Eloise said that she'd run off to find her father, and you had sent men after her but they hadn't yet returned. Nothing was said to implicate us. Instead, she inferred we were her family now."

Maeve considered me.

"Your lie of omission cannot go unpunished. It's a pity about the spell. A beating would have been easier for you."

"If anything happens to Kaven, the Prince will—.

"It's not Kaven who will suffer. Remember, your choices brought you to this fate."

Her amulet flashed brightly, and an abyss followed, swallowing me whole.

CHAPTER SIX

THE OVERWHELMING NEED TO VOMIT JERKED ME UPRIGHT. Turning my head, I gagged once then emptied my stomach into the mud and straw. Despite that, the nausea didn't fade. Instead, my head thumped in time with my pulse as I gasped for breath.

I closed my eyes against the light of day, trying to find a moment's ease from the constant roiling of my stomach, but there was none. I continued to gag as I turned to my side and got to my knees. The ringing in my ears grew in volume as I tried to stand, only to stumble to my knees again.

Everything hurt as if I'd been beaten again. I blinked slowly, trying to clear my mind of the pain as I inspected my arms for injuries. However, I was too covered with filth to see. Gagging again, which had nothing to do with whatever was covering me, I tried to wipe my hands and arms clean. My efforts only made matters worse.

I struggled to my feet, panting, and noted that I was encumbered only by the shaking of my limbs. Confused, I glanced down at myself and stumbled at the sight of bare, dirty legs and torso. I touched my soot-covered stomach, trying to understand as I looked around.

The small dead-end alley in which I stood was stacked with broken barrels and old straw. Nothing looked familiar. Frowning, I struggled to remember how I'd gotten here or why I was naked. I recalled the dinner with the Prince then—

A tug in my middle almost brought me to my knees again. My stomach heaved, and I coughed on bile. The burn in my throat was barely noticeable amidst all the other pain I suffered, and my vision swam dizzily. However, the urge to move, to start walking home, had me struggling to my feet once again.

"Ho! What do we have here, lads? This little bit seems to have lost her way."

I turned and found three men in the entrance to the alley. While the lead man leered at my filth-coated breasts with open fascination, the other two did not look tempted. Still, I used my hands in a feeble attempt to shield myself from their view.

"I ain't touching that," one said, sniffing. "She's covered in pig shite."

"A bit of water will clean her up."

My stomach heaved. Whether from the thought of these men touching me or whatever ailed me, I emptied my stomach again.

"Please," I gasped. "Help me."

One of them swore.

"She's sick."

Something hit my shoulder. I grunted as the impact knocked me off balance then lifted my head to see one of the men bending down for another rock. The rocks wouldn't hurt me, and even as wretched as I was, I knew I couldn't let them discover that. Such a mysterious ability would only bring much more unwanted attention to me.

I lurched toward the opening of the alley where they stood, needing to escape. They moved back as if being near me would cause them to fall ill, too. However, I knew better. The illness I felt was the magical pull to return home.

I rounded the corner, emerging onto the road. My eyes swept the area. I didn't know where I was. Looking up, I spotted the castle's turrets in the distance. I was in Towdown. How had I even left home?

Maeve's final words in the carriage came back to me. She'd done this.

Another pull knocked me forward. I put my hand on the nearest building to brace myself.

"Go on! Take your sickness from here. We don't want the likes of you in Towdown."

A rock hit me in the back as did something else firm

and wet. I pitched forward, not to escape them but to make my way home to end my suffering.

People stopped to stare at me as I made slow progress through the streets. Mothers covered their children's eyes, a reminder that I wore nothing. Men stared, either laughing or making lewd comments. I kept my hands covering my front, only sacrificing what little modesty that gained to prevent myself from falling.

All the while, my tormentors stayed behind me, driving me forward with whatever they could find to throw at me. I didn't need to stop and look where I was. Though I had no idea, the pull kept me moving in the correct direction.

I turned a corner and found myself at the edge of the market district. The back alleys that I'd traversed so far had kept me from drawing a large crowd, something that would certainly happen if I went through the market. I turned around and attempted to take another route.

The men following me threw even more at me, trying to turn me back toward the market. But, I lifted my arms and ducked down, determined to find another way even as the pull caused me to gag and made my eyes water.

Winning my way to another side road, I continued on.

"Stop," someone yelled from ahead.

There wasn't a way I could stop even if I wanted to listen. My insides felt like they were on fire, now. I had to keep moving.

"Throw one more thing," the voice shouted, "and I'll find where you live and burn it to the ground."

I slowed and looked up, shocked by the vehemence in the words.

Ahead, I saw the backside of Crumbs and Casks with Alfie standing by the rear door. He wasn't looking at me but at those that followed me.

"Go on! Leave the woman alone."

"She has a sickness," one of the men said.

"So did half the town not more than a week ago. No one used stones to cure it then, yet here we are, hale and hardy. Not everything is as it seems."

Grumbles came from behind me. Then silence.

I stumbled forward, grateful for even that small bit of a reprieve. Alfie rushed toward me, gripping my arms to help steady me as he guided me to a bench near the back door.

As soon as I sat, he pulled off his shirt.

"Put this on. I'll see if I can find a cloak or something, too."

I took the shirt with trembling hands and looked up at him. After all the years he and his friends had tormented Kellen and me, I never would have thought to receive any kindness from him.

His eyes widened as we stared at each other.

"No. This is enough," I said, standing. "Thank you."

"Wha—?"

Movement to my right caught my attention. I caught a glimpse of a familiar cloak before it disappeared. I continued to stare, waiting, and was rewarded when Porcia peeked around the corner at me. My stomach twisted.

"Should I call for a carriage?"

I leaned in and purposely threw up on him. He cried out in disgust but didn't move. Lifting my head, I looked him in the eye.

"Run," I whispered fiercely under the guise of wiping my mouth.

His eyes widened, and he ran back inside. I pivoted and stumbled in the direction of the estate as I tugged his shirt over my filthy body. Maeve meant this to be a punishment and wouldn't like that I now had a shirt. I smiled slightly, not caring.

The agony tearing at my insides did not ease with each step. Instead, the urgency to get home only grew more intense. My shuffling gait became a trundling jog.

When I reached the edge of town, Porcia called my name softly. I stopped and looked back at her. She waved me to a path between two houses. It was the opposite way I needed to go, but I followed her regardless. She was here for a reason. When we reached the backyard, several buckets of water waited along with a clean dress.

"Rinse what you can and dress. Mama doesn't want you returning to the estate like this."

I stripped from Alfie's shirt and dumped the buckets over my head in quick succession. They didn't clean me. Using the shirt, I dried myself, spreading the muck more than removing it from my skin, then tugged the dress over my head only to promptly throw up on myself. I looked down at the yellow stain, wondering how I still had anything in me.

"Mama will not be pleased," Porcia said. "You're no better than you were before."

"Her action is what brought this fate," I rasped, pivoting to start home.

Porcia walked with me in silence. I noted the way she wrung her hands as we walked the road home.

"Why you?" I asked.

"Because I ate everything I was served last night," she said.

I grunted, not understanding or truly caring what the reason was. As we neared the drive, I started to jog again. Porcia panted trying to keep up. The pain intensified until the last moment when I stepped over the estate's boundary. All the pain and sickness vanished. I stopped and took a deep, cleansing breath.

"Come, Mama is waiting."

"Let her wait," I said, moving toward the shed. At the horse trough, I stripped from the dress and sank into the water. Ducking under, I let it cover my head, cooling me and my rage. Naked, and covered in filth, I'd been driven through town by vicious men. Had the spell not protected me—

I screamed under the water and scrubbed at myself.

When I emerged, I felt no calmer.

A low chuckle reached my ears, and I looked up at Seth

who leaned against the side of the shed near the end of the trough.

"Can't say I'll mind having to change out the water for the privilege of this view."

I glanced around and saw Porcia was missing.

"You'd better run, Seth," I said. "When Mama comes, she will not like what you're doing."

He smirked, glanced at the house, and paled.

I followed his gaze and saw Maeve standing in the now open door.

Seth nodded his head at her then went back into the depths of the shed.

While she crossed the yard, I exited the trough as gracefully as possible and looked down at myself. Although the water running down my skin wasn't clear, dirt no longer coated me.

"Have you no shame?" Maeve demanded angrily as she reached me. "A proper young lady does not bathe in the open."

"The buckets of water in town didn't clean me, and Porcia said you would be disappointed by my filth. Disappointing you so soon after my latest punishment didn't seem wise. And given that I just walked naked through town, I didn't think I was still a proper young lady. I apologize for misunderstanding." I kept my tone neutral, devoid of any emotion.

Maeve picked up my discarded dress and threw it at me. "Put it on."

I tugged the dress over my head and met her gaze. Anger rolled off of her, unmasked and unbridled. It paled in comparison to mine.

She took a deep breath and regained control.

"What if we'd had company, Eloise? What if the Prince was here to call upon us?"

I said nothing, and she sighed.

"You need to think before you act. While I appreciate your attempt to please me, it had the opposite effect."

"Sorry, Mama."

"Come," she said.

I followed her through the main doors of the house.

"Catherine! Heather!" Maeve yelled.

My eyes rounded, and I stared at Maeve in horror. What had she done? Were my friends alive? How? I saw them die with my own eyes.

Two women I didn't know hurried from the dining room and curtsied to Maeve.

"Yes, mistress?" the older one said.

"This is my daughter, Eloise. Eloise, this is Heather, and that is Catherine."

"The same names?" I said, unable to conceal my pain.

"I'm tired of learning new names. With the rate the maids leave this house, I thought it more expeditious to use the names we already know. At least until we know if this pair will last longer."

I heard the threat there. I wanted to kill her. Slowly. Painfully. The need burned a well inside of me. It was good and deep, hidden from my expression, but still there despite any word I might utter.

"You said no more maids."

"Honestly, Eloise. I don't know why you are so against help. Catherine and Heather are lovely women."

"We will do our best to see to your every need," Heather said.

"We truly want to stay," Catherine added.

I looked at them, closing myself off from the pain— past, present, and any that might find me in the future because of them.

"I'm so glad to hear that," Maeve said. "Because Eloise has had a bit of a mishap on the road and needs to bathe quite desperately. The tub is in the kitchen. Please see to it."

They both nodded and hurried off.

"Come, Eloise. There is more," Maeve said, heading toward the sitting room.

I followed her at a subdued paced.

Inside the room, I found Porcia and Cecilia already waiting.

"Sit," Maeve directed. She waited for me to comply then looked at Porcia. "Tell me everything."

Porcia recounted my experience in town, sparing no detail, right down to the rock that hit my tailbone and the clump of horse shit that someone had managed to lob at my head with dreadful accuracy.

"Perhaps the wash in the trough was a good decision," Maeve murmured with a glance at me.

Then Porcia shared the help I received.

"Did he recognize you?" Maeve asked.

"The entire time I walked, the spell worked its magic, making my ears ring and the world around me tip and tilt as I stumbled and vomited everywhere. Nothing made sense but finding my way home."

"Do not think to withhold information from me, again," she warned. "Did he recognize you?"

"If he did, I wouldn't have noticed. I vomited on him the moment he asked if he could call a carriage for me."

Maeve looked at Porcia.

"It's true. And he never called her by name, nor she by his."

Maeve remained quiet for a moment.

"The next time you defy me, I will have men hold you down and violate you in the most horrific ways so it haunts your dreams until your dying day. Yet, they will leave your precious virginity intact. Do you understand me?"

I swallowed hard and nodded, unable to speak past the lump in my throat.

"Good." She went to the desk and retrieved a bit of parchment that she held out to me. "While you were away, another invitation arrived. Written by the Prince himself."

The invitation formally requested the Cartwright family's presence at the next ball, which was to be masked, and promised the attendance of Drisdall's most suitable unmarried men in good standing with the Crown. The end of the note stated, "I am looking forward to Eloise's attendance." It was signed Prince Greydon, House of Drisdall, in an almost illegible scrawl.

"You want me to attend the ball?" I asked.

Cecilia snorted, and Maeve smiled.

"Of course not. You've proven yourself incapable of making proper choices when left on your own. And you would be on your own at the ball, dancing with the Prince. No, as it's a masked ball and you and Cecilia are so similar in appearance, Cecilia will present herself as you if she must. You will stay here, where you belong until you are needed. After the ball, Cecilia will tell you everything so that you may discuss it as if you were there."

I glanced at Cecilia. She smiled at me. Was she even thinking Maeve's plan through?

"The Prince has spoken to me. Surely he will recognize a difference in our voices, regardless of the mask you wear. And if you are to be me, how will you win the Prince's affection as your own?"

"She doesn't need to speak," Maeve said, answering for her. "And she will win the Prince's affection outside of the ballroom. Starting today, you will walk with your sister. Twice a day. If you happen upon Kaven, you will speak well of your sister's many accomplishments. You will see to it that the Prince's curiosity is piqued enough that we receive another dinner invitation. This time because of Cecilia."

"Yes, Mama."

"Good. Now, go bathe. I cannot tolerate another moment of the smell emanating from you."

"Thank you for watching over me, Porcia," I said with a nod before leaving the room.

Instead of going to the kitchen, I went to my room. The water would take a while to heat and the tub even longer to fill. Rather than sit in the kitchen and risk learning more about the new maids, I sequestered myself in my attic space. I roamed the furniture placements and thought over the last two days.

The result of the dinner with the Prince could have been worse. Rather than exposing that we'd already met, he could have taken one look at Cecilia and fallen in love. As it was, he spent the majority of his time focused on me. His attention was another layer of safety for me.

Maeve believed the Prince's interest in me nothing more than a passing curiosity brought about because of Kaven's lofty esteem. I wasn't so sure. I'd noted the way Kaven frowned at the way the Prince touched me. Why frown if it was completely proper? Kaven must have sensed something I had not. He was, after all, very close to the Prince. Which also created a layer of protection for Kaven. His potential usefulness in swaying the Prince's opinion of Cecilia would keep Kaven reasonably safe for a time, no matter my behavior. And that explained why I'd walked the streets of Towdown naked instead of Kaven bearing the brunt of Maeve's wrath at my omission of the Prince's presence.

It was a dangerous game I played but no more dangerous than the one Maeve played.

The latest invitation to the ball worried me. The Prince was expecting me. I had no doubt that Cecilia and Maeve had a convincing plan for how Cecilia would portray me, or they wouldn't attempt such a thing. And by using the Prince's interest in me, it would put Cecilia that much closer to me.

A thought dawned, and I wanted to groan.

Cecilia would be close enough to crack the amulet. With it cracked, Cecilia wouldn't need to speak to win over the Prince's heart. It wouldn't matter who the Prince thought he was dancing with.

In agitation, I continued to pace around the room. How could I possibly stop them? If today had taught me anything, it was that I would never be able to leave the estate with Maeve's spell binding me to this place.

I found myself standing near the chimney and looked up at the spot where I'd hidden the mask the tree had given me. It had given me what I would need to attend the ball before I'd even known it would be a masked ball. If the tree could do that, surely it could also provide a cure to the spell holding me here. Why else give me the mask if not to attend?

"Miss Eloise," a voice called. "Your bath is ready."

"Coming."

CHAPTER SEVEN

I tipped my head up to the sun and let the light warm my face. Around me, the birds and other creatures were silent.

"I'm tired of sitting here," Cecilia said. "Let's walk toward the Retreat."

"You know I can't."

"What I know is that Mama gave you a task, and you're not doing it."

"I am doing it. Kaven finds me. I don't find him."

"That's the most ridiculous thing I've heard."

I shrugged my shoulders and looked out over Towdown. With Cecilia constantly in tow, I hadn't returned to the clearing and Mother's grave. At least, not for any extended period of time. Instead, I went everywhere else on the estate, even going so far as to walk the pig in the woods along the ridge. She hadn't liked that because of the pig and the distance from the Retreat. The memory of her annoyance then made it harder not to smile as she glared at me now.

"I'm returning to the house. The last four days have been a fruitless waste of my time." She stood and stormed off.

Our time together hadn't been entirely fruitless, though. Not for me, anyway. In the last few days, I'd enjoyed more time outside in the trees I loved than I had in previous weeks. And, I was entirely grateful that Kaven hadn't once happened upon us.

As the bird song slowly emerged and grew in volume, I stood and hurriedly shook out my skirts to follow after Cecilia. I knew the sound would draw Kaven to me, and I didn't want that to happen.

"Good afternoon, Miss Eloise," Catherine said with forced cheer as I entered the kitchen.

"Is it?" I answered coldly.

Cecilia narrowed her eyes at me from her place at the table as I removed my cloak and left the trio in the kitchen.

I hated that I treated the maids so coldly, but I believed my friendship and fondness for the true Catherine and Heather had been what led to their inevitable demise. After all, their deaths had been yet another means of punishing me. It was safer to act coldly toward the new maids than to form any bond. I wouldn't give Maeve more reason to hurt those who served us.

Heading for the stairs, I returned to my room as I did

every afternoon, now. The day after my walk through town, I'd learned that Maeve had spun a lovely tale about me to the new help. One where I was an errant, misbehaved child, who cared little about how my actions might hurt myself or others. My cold behavior only gave more credence to her explanation and made Maeve's nightly routine of locking me in my room more befitting.

I minded neither the lock nor the lie. Both kept Catherine and Heather safer.

I roamed my room, walking amongst the memories of my past, as I waited for the knock on my door to signal that one of my sisters was bringing up a tray. Afterward, I would eat alone and listen for the carriage to leave. The nightly pilgrimage my unwanted family took to join the festivities of the lower class outside the castle was a routine they had been following for the last four days.

When the knock came, I was already sitting at my table.

"Good evening, sister," Cecilia said.

I rolled my eyes before I turned to face her.

"Good evening, sister. It's nice spending so much time with you and then having you wait on me like a commoner."

Her eyes narrowed on me, and she dropped the tray the few inches to the table, letting the juice from the beans splash on the wooden surface.

"Whatever is the matter, sister?" I asked with sugary sweetness.

"I will never be common."

"Oh? Tell me again how the common folk view you."

She leaned toward me.

"When I am queen, I will see you flayed and hung. Your body will rot at the end of a rope and no one will care because everyone you love is dead."

"But I love you, sister. And Porcia. And Mama. We're a family. Family doesn't hurt one another."

She bared her teeth at me.

"You know nothing about family."

I leaned back in my chair.

"Teasing aside, how are things progressing in Towdown? Do you think you're getting any closer to winning the Prince's favor since we're having no luck here?"

She studied me for a moment, likely trying to gauge my sincerity. It was a game I'd been playing with her since Maeve forbade her from striking out against me. I provoked her to the point she wanted to cause me physical harm, then I spoke nicely to her as if I cared.

"Of course, I'm closer. Despite your lack of help. It's not only the people who are taking note of me but the palace guards as well. I'm sure word is spreading."

I felt certain it was, too, and that worried me.

"Sit," I said, nudging out a chair with my foot. "I miss conversation while eating."

"I cannot. Mama is waiting below. We're to go to town again tonight."

I glanced at her dress, a deeply-hued frock.

"You should change into something lighter. Although it won't highlight your beauty, it will help you stand out more against the dull colors the commoners use."

"I want to blend with them, though."

I gave an indolent shrug.

"You've already worked to make them accept you as their own. Now, you need to stand out in the eyes of the Prince should he be walking the parapets. Which I believe he will tonight. Why else would Kaven be absent so long if not for an extended stay at the castle with the Prince."

Cecilia smoothed her hands over her dress.

"If you're wrong..."

"I'm not wrong about the people viewing you differently. If you've truly won their acceptance, the color or style of your dress won't matter so long as you continue to treat them as you have. However, I can make no promises about the Prince's appearance tonight. That is only speculation."

She reluctantly thanked me for my advice before leaving me alone. I smiled and quickly ate my food.

From the small window on the other side of the attic, I watched the wagon pull away from the house. Walking the length of the attic, I listened to Catherine and Heather move about below. When they finished turning down the beds for the night and returned to the first level, I retrieved the master key that Cecilia had been too blind to notice when she first ruined my attic sanctuary.

As soon as the house quieted, I carried my tray to the

foot of the stairs, where I typically left it, and let myself out. Sneaking from the house wasn't hard. I'd wandered the rooms a few times the previous night just to test Catherine and Heather's awareness. The trick would be returning before Maeve and my stepsisters, for they would most certainly note me coming in through the front door.

Once outside, I breathed in deeply of the night air and made for the tree. I desperately needed Mother's help to understand how I was supposed to leave the estate to attend the ball with the mask it had given me. Cecilia was indeed winning over too many people with her efforts. Even Catherine and Heather liked her.

The weak moonlight guided my passage along the path. Even though I struggled to see, the creatures around me had no issue recognizing me. The moment I sat on the bench, they started making noise enough to wake the dead. I hoped Kaven was far from here and unlikely to hear—

"Eloise?"

My heart leapt, and I struggled to contain the joy I felt at his presence.

"You shouldn't be here."

"I couldn't stay away. It's been driving me mad that Cecilia has been a constant presence at your side for the last four days. I've wanted to speak with you."

"And she wanted to speak with you."

"Me? Why?" he asked, crossing the clearing.

"Because she has seen how you can influence the Prince's opinion. She wants to impress him."

"I see."

"I doubt you do. What were you thinking?" I asked as he sat beside me.

"At what point?"

"When you stated your interest in me to my stepmother. And, what are your intentions even? You haven't yet told me."

He chuckled softly and took one of my hands.

"I was thinking that I'm tired of trying to be patient. I want to marry you."

I snorted.

"You barely know me."

He laughed.

"That's a problem that marriage will quickly fix."

I opened my mouth to argue, but he took the opportunity to kiss me fiercely. I melted against the onslaught, able to do little else. My head swam, and my hands settled on his chest. When he pulled away, he grinned down at me.

"I've never felt, for anyone, what I feel for you. When we're together, I'm alive. You challenge me to be better than I am. And I want to be. Because of you. Yes, I want to marry you, Eloise. Yes, I'm willing to wait. But I don't want to. If you feel we don't know each other well enough, it only means we need to spend more time together. I will call on you again tomorrow."

His words penetrated the fog in my mind.

"No." I pushed against his chest, winning some space.

"Your first attempt didn't progress very well. Why do you think the second would be any different?"

He frowned slightly, his frustration showing.

"Tell me what to do, then. How do I win your hand?"

"You don't," I said, pulling away from him. "I'm not supposed to be seeing you. I snuck from the house while my family is in town. If Mama finds out I spent time alone with you in the woods..."

His expression hardened.

"What? What will she do?"

"She will rush her plans for me. I do not want to be like the Prince, forced to marry a stranger within a month's time."

He considered me silently for a long moment.

"That is exactly why I need to persuade her that I am a good match for you."

"You can't."

"Why not?"

I looked up into his beautiful blue eyes and saw his determination and stubbornness. Both would get him killed. I knew then that I needed to let him go. But how?

His expression softened.

"Don't," he said softly.

"Don't what?"

"Find a reason to push me away."

My brows rose in surprise.

"I can read you better than you realize, Eloise. When you feel threatened, you don't run; you fight back. Why does marrying me scare you? I know my employ isn't it. You've made your stance on Drisdall's social system very clear. You see everyone as equals. If I am your equal, why do you want to run at the thought of marrying me? Is it my visage? Many a maid has told me I'm handsome."

I snorted again.

"Please. It is not your face or form. You know very well a flash of your dimple would send most females to their knees."

He grinned wickedly.

"You on your knees before me is an image that will keep me up for many nights to come."

I sighed.

"I cannot marry you, Kaven. It's as simple as that."

He studied me for a moment.

"Now or ever?"

I hesitated. It would be safer to say forever, but my heart wouldn't allow it.

"For now," I admitted softly. "I need you to stop pressing the matter for now."

"That I can do. But with great reluctance."

A small smile curved his lips before he kissed me once more.

"Tell me that I will see you the day after tomorrow," he said.

I blinked up at him, confused.

"You have no earnest need to see me tomorrow?" I asked.

"Oh, I do. But I especially want to see you at the ball. I want to hold you close and dance with you. I want the world to know you'll be mine. Eventually."

"You want me to attend a ball where the guest of honor is meant to select a bride from the women assembled? Don't you think that's a bit presumptuous? After all, Prince Greydon seems to have an interest in me."

"He does indeed," Kaven said in all seriousness.

"I think it best that I stay home. I wouldn't want to start a quarrel between the two of you."

A small smile tilted the corner of Kaven's mouth.

"He and I quarrel more often than I would like," he admitted.

"You quarrel with the Prince? Is that wise?"

"What happened to your thoughts of equality?"

"I believe in equality, but it's very apparent that the Prince does not."

"How so?"

"Only maids in good standing with the Crown may attend the ball. Those who are not in good standing are forced to watch from outside the palace gates. That is a definitive inequality if ever there was one."

"It's to protect the Prince. There is a threat to this kingdom, one that's already taken far too much life."

"I understand that well. The loss of his first wife truly necessitates care. But why do you think the threat is only possible from those in a lower class? What if I were the threat? You've never met me before. How do you know I wasn't the one responsible for the Prince's wife?"

"First, you're not old enough. Second, I believe the true threat would use a level of subtly of which you are not capable. After all, you hit me with a rock."

My mouth dropped open, and he leaned forward to kiss the tip of my nose.

"That was when I saw you for what you are."

"What am I?"

"An amazing woman worth knowing. One whose threat comes from her sharp wit and tongue, not magic. For if you had magic, you would have either used it against me then, or you would have never confronted me in the first place."

"I think the rock addled your mind."

He laughed, the deep sound making my stomach tighten. His humor faded as he looked at me and he leaned forward once more to capture my lips. It wasn't the kiss to show his affection and delight in me as it had been before. Nor was it one with the urgency of longing after an extended absence. Instead, his lips claimed mine with a barely restrained hunger that sent my pulse racing.

I grasped his shoulders, anchoring myself as my world spun. His arms slipped around me, holding me tightly, and the heat from the palms of his hands scorched my sides. He toyed with me, teasing me with his tongue as he pressed his chest to mine. The world tilted, and I found myself laying back on the bench. When he lifted his head for a moment, I panted for breath only to moan when his lips found the column of my throat.

"You call to me like no other," he whispered against my skin. "You are my shield and my light."

I barely heard him. He was kissing his way down to my neckline. My heart fluttered in my chest, anticipating what he would do next. There was a tug at my dress a moment before the night air cooled the heated skin of my breasts.

Kaven groaned and set his mouth on one peak. The heat of his tongue undid me. I gasped and arched underneath him.

"Eloise." He slowly kissed his way upward again, his lips once more claiming mine.

I lost myself. I would have done anything and everything he wanted at that moment, and I would have known nothing but joy. However, he abandoned me just as the kiss heated to a fevered state.

I blinked at the stars above, trying to breathe and form a coherent thought. When I realized he wasn't returning to me, I sat up and looked around. He paced the far side of the clearing.

"Kaven?"

"I'm tired of this game," he said harshly.

Hurt consumed me.

"I didn't know it was a game to you." I sat up and straightened my gown. Before I finished, he knelt in front of me and stopped my hands.

"You are not a game. What I feel for you is not a game.

I'm frustrated with the waiting. With wanting you so much. Forgive me for speaking so bitterly. The vexation I feel has nothing to do with you and everything to do with anyone who is delaying the time when we can finally be together."

I frowned at him and smoothed my fingers along the light whiskers coating his jaw and cheeks. The same whiskers that had so nicely abraded my skin.

"Perhaps, it would be best if we did not see each other until such a time as we can truly be together."

His expression darkened, and I leaned forward to kiss him gently.

"You are not the only one to suffer when we meet like this," I added softly.

He sighed and rested his forehead against mine.

"As you wish."

CHAPTER EIGHT

THE TIME I'D SPENT WITH KAVEN THE NIGHT BEFORE LAST consumed me, and I blindly stared at the small circle of light on the floor, dreading the conclusion to which I'd arrived. I needed to give myself to Kaven while attempting to win the heart of the Prince. It sounded like madness, but I knew it was the only way to ensure Maeve would not win.

I considered again Rose's words to me. *All curses have an end. Once the goal is met, the curse will break on its own.* By winning the Prince's heart, I felt certain the spell holding me silent would break. With the spell broken, I could condemn Maeve for her actions against the Crown. I only hoped that once the threat was removed, the Prince would understand my deception in marrying him as an impure woman and release me from our vows. If not, I would endure whatever punishment he saw fit, knowing that I'd kept the kingdom, and Kaven, safe.

If I couldn't win the Prince's heart, my impurity when taking Cecilia's place in the marriage bed would be noticed, and the whole deception would be exposed. It was a dangerous risk. Cecilia could lie and say I'd tricked my way into his bed, and I would be able to say nothing to implicate Maeve. That plan was, however, a last resort. I still hoped to end Maeve's attempt to gain access to the Crown by exposing Cecilia and Porcia for what they really were. I wasn't quite sure how, though.

"Eloise, the seamstress is here for the final fittings," Maeve called to me from my doorway. "She's requested your assistance."

I sighed and descended the stairs.

"You've been unusually quiet," Maeve commented as she walked with me.

"Boredom and seclusion are dulling my conversation skills."

"Then it is a good thing you can assist today."

"It most certainly is, Mama."

Since keeping me locked in the attic, Maeve spent very little time with me. I'd thought, perhaps, that meant her focus had shifted to Cecilia...until she spoke.

"Your behavior is greatly improved, Eloise. I have a mind to request a dress be made for you for the final ball."

I looked up sharply to see if she was serious. If she meant for me to openly contend for the Prince's favor, it would make my effort to win him over that much harder because of Cecilia's inevitable interference.

"I will need to test your loyalty, of course."

My stomach tightened with fear.

"I would prefer to continue to support Cecilia in her endeavor to win the Prince's affection, Mama. She's worked so hard for this chance," I quickly said.

"Yet, she's continually failing where you succeeded with little effort. The mirror showed us that you would be his first choice. I think it's time to acknowledge that."

My mind raced, but I could say nothing in return as we entered the sitting room just then.

Cecilia stood upon the hemming stool. The angry light in her eyes made me wonder if she'd overheard Maeve's suggestion.

"Please repeat what you just told me," Cecilia said to Madame Blye, who kneeled at Cecilia's feet.

"The new proclamation announced at the festivities last night has set Towdown on its ear. I haven't slept since the night before last."

The dark circles under her eyes gave credence to her words.

"Get on with it," Cecilia said with cold impatience.

"Every maid—be she fair, in good standing with the Crown, or not—is invited to tonight's ball. It will be a crush." She waved at me. "Don't just stand there, girl. Help me with this hem. I have other dresses to alter yet this day."

I hurried forward and took the pin cushion from her. She had barely handed it off when she continued with her story.

"Every maid, and I mean each one, is preparing to make their way to the castle tonight. I can't imagine how the Royal family hopes to accommodate everyone. What with all the eligible men the Prince decreed would attend last week. Those who can't afford a new dress are handing over their coppers for pretty masks to match their best frocks."

She made quick work of the hemming while she spoke then stood to tug and smooth.

"Perfection," she announced. "Some of my best work. You'll even outshine my own gown tonight."

"You're going?" I couldn't hold back my surprise.

"I'm of an age and unmarried. Of course, I'm going."

"I meant no disrespect."

"Then perhaps you shouldn't speak."

Cecilia smirked at my reprimand, and Maeve said nothing.

Once Porcia's dress was fitted and the seamstress left, I spent the next several hours attending to Cecilia and Porcia. Scenting their baths after the maids hauled the water. Brushing out their hair before the fire. Helping tighten and tuck so they looked flawless in their gowns. Then, assisting Maeve with styling their hair.

"Look at these matching shoes," Cecilia said, preening in front of her mirror. "There are even more beads sewn to them than the last pair."

I dutifully looked at the shoes.

"They are lovely."

"Perhaps, once I'm queen," she said, "I'll give you this dress and these shoes."

"Thank you."

Maeve entered Cecilia's bedroom, her gaze pinning me.

"You prematurely thank your sister. She hasn't even managed to catch the Prince's notice yet."

Cecilia's smile vanished.

"I'm certain I will tonight."

"Tonight? When the room is sure to be crowded with five times as many maids as it was with the previous ball? You are neither simple nor a fool, so stop acting like one. I'm of a mind to have you strip from those clothes and give them to your sister."

I quickly stepped forward.

"No, Mama. Please."

Maeve looked at me, a pleased smile on her face.

"It is good of you to support your sister. Be sure you do not do so blindly."

"Yes, Mama."

She gave a stern look to Cecilia.

"Come along. It's time you prove yourself."

Maeve swept from the room. When I glanced at Cecilia, her face was flushed, and she stared at the vacant opening. If she'd wanted to flay and hang me for my rash words, I could only imagine what she wanted to do to her mother just then. I kept silent, too shrewd to draw attention to myself.

Without a glance my way, she left the room. I breathed

a sigh of relief, and quietly followed. Maeve waited in the hall, the key in her hand.

"Goodnight, Mama," I said to her.

"Goodnight, my dear one. We will see the dressmaker tomorrow."

My chest tightened with worry, and I hurried upstairs. How did she believe she would control me if I—

"You cannot be serious," Cecilia's voice echoed through the far heat vent.

I moved closer on silent feet and caught the end of Maeve's response.

"—opportunity for what it is. The Prince is already fond of her. Let him think he's wedding her. However, it will be you speaking the vows."

"You still mean for me to be queen? Not Eloise?"

"Eloise will never be queen."

I waited for Cecilia to repeat her question about being queen, to demand the truth, but she remained quiet. Could she truly be that blind to her mother's true nature?

"We've delayed long enough. Come. We have a Prince to protect," Maeve said.

"How many maids from the mirror are still alive?" Cecilia asked.

"Three before you. Five after Porcia. But only two will attend."

"How do you know?"

"Six can no longer see."

The satisfaction in Maeve's words filled me with horror, and I covered my mouth with my hand.

"Thank you, Mama," Cecilia said happily.

I listened to their footsteps fade as I stood near the vent. She'd blinded girls just to prevent them from attending a ball? Who could be so cruel?

After the carriage left, I once again used the key to sneak from the house. This time, I had the mask tucked into my bodice. Although the creatures greeted me with their typical noise, I knew Kaven wouldn't be there to interrupt. Which was exactly why I'd waited until tonight when he too would be at the ball.

When I reached the clearing, I went to the tree and held up the mask.

"The mask alone will not help me win the Prince, for I cannot cross the estate's boundaries to attend the ball. Will you help me, please? I must win the Prince's affection. I must wed the Prince. There is no other way."

The white bird chirped from its perch, and the branches trembled, sending a shower of petals down around me. I looked up to see a shimmer of silvery blue light. It grew in shape and size, swirling and twirling in a sparkle of magnificent light until it solidified into cloth. The fabric fell in a tumble, but I recognized it for what it was. I caught the dress and held it up. The creation of magic and beauty glistened in the moonlight. Flower petals dotted the bodice and skirt. It was simple in its beauty and so much more.

I looked up at the tree.

"Will the dress help me leave?"

Again, the branches shook. This time, twin balls of light appeared. They glowed brighter than the dress had yet were much smaller. The bird sang a sweet song as the shape of two shoes gradually formed then fell to the ground with a thunk. I picked them up to see they were made of silver and glass. The slippers caught and reflected moonlight, no matter which way I turned them.

"These are beautiful, and I'm truly grateful. But, the mask didn't allow me to leave. Are you sure these will?"

The tree groaned, and a rending crack echoed through the clearing as more petals fell. Quickly, a split emerged down the middle of the beautiful tree. As I watched, each half bent further from the other. A shimmer began to grow in the space. Like Maeve's mirror, this shimmer started cloudy. But, unlike the mirror, the surface cleared into the image of a perfectly manicured garden.

A breeze swept over me, warm and scented with honeysuckle. I inhaled deeply and studied the image.

"It's not like the mirror at all, is it?" I said. "It's a means for me to leave the estate. The honeysuckle I smell is from that garden, isn't it?"

The bird stopped singing and tapped the wood several times before looking at me.

"I don't understand."

It tapped the wood again. Twelve times.

I still didn't understand but decided not to waste any more time. It was already well after eight.

Picking up the shoes, I slipped them onto my feet. Then, after a quick look around, I changed from my gown to the one given to me by the tree. Finally, I tied on my mask.

"How do I look?" I asked.

The bird sang loudly, and the song was echoed around me as dozens of birds flew from the trees. I wasn't afraid of them, but such a swarm flying straight at my head made me cringe and duck. However, they didn't do more than peck at my hair as they flew close for several moments then returned to their trees.

I reached up and touched my hair, feeling flower petals and ringlets held up by twigs and vines.

The bird tapped the wood again. Twelve times.

"You're right. There's no time to worry about hair. Thank you for your help. I love you, Mother."

I walked toward the shimmer and stepped between the split branches into a pool of water. Looking back, I saw the shimmer closing and felt a stab of worry. However, no pain or sickness affected me.

When the shimmer vanished, I saw nothing but the other side of the pond disappearing into the darkness. I looked around at the garden. Tall hedges blocked this part in. Music and the light of the castle beckoned ahead. I took a step forward and heard a splash. Lifting my skirts, I looked at light reflecting off my glass slippers as I walked on top of the water. Beneath me, I watched the fish swim.

"Remarkable," I said softly.

However, when I reached dry ground, trepidation filled my veins. The tree had given me what I needed to escape the estate without pain. But, could Maeve still sense me?

Knowing I didn't have time to ponder the consequences if she did, I hurried toward the castle, weaving my way out of the dark section of the garden to the light where several couples mingled. Steps led from the garden to the ballroom where strains of music floated on the air. Inside, I could see the swirling colors of numerous gowns.

"You are a vision," an unfamiliar voice said.

I turned to look at the masked man beside me. His jacket was clean but threadbare, and his mask a creation of common raven feathers. A group of gowned women stood in a cluster not far from where we stood and whispered while watching us.

"Please honor me with a dance," he said, earnestly. "I promised my mother I would dance at least once before returning home."

"Only once?"

He flushed slightly as the girls laughed, having heard my question, and I understood his dilemma.

"The honor is mine, good sir," I said with a curtsy. He bowed hastily and offered his arm. I spoke softly as we ascended the stairs.

"That should put them in their place," I said. "Ignore

the ones who measure a man's value in the cut of his cloth. They will never make suitable wives. Instead, find one who will look you in the eye and measure your worth by your actions."

We stopped at the edge of the dance floor and faced each other.

"And how do you measure men?" he asked.

I smiled, knowing the answer he hoped for.

"I don't. Not yet. Perhaps I will when I'm looking for a husband."

His disappointment was brief as he offered me his hand then swept me onto the dance floor. After only a moment, he stepped on my foot and cringed. I laughed lightly.

"I assure you, my shoes are sturdy and you will cause me no harm."

"I'm sorry. I only learned the dance this week."

"Your mother?" I asked.

"Yes."

"She's a marvelous teacher if you're doing this well after so little time."

He chuckled.

"I've barely slept for all the dancing I've done. I'm not the only one. Most of my friends here are the same. Not all of them made the promise I did. Bast—beg your pardon—my friends are stuffing their faces at the table instead of dancing."

As I swept around the room, I noticed a few women

watching us. Like my partner, they wore simpler clothes and masks.

"That might change when they see the success of your dancing."

"Do not call this a success too quickly. We should wait to see if you can walk after the song ends."

I laughed.

"So be it," I said.

When the song finished, I smiled at my partner and curtsied.

"I believe you will find another willing partner or two near the wall just to the side."

"Thank you, miss..."

"Since it's a masked ball, I'd prefer to keep my name to myself."

He chuckled, bowed, and left me just as the music started up again.

"You look in need of another partner," a familiar voice said.

Heart racing, I turned toward Kaven. But it wasn't the Kaven I knew. Gone were the cocky hat with the king's insignia and worn jacket. In their place, his light brown hair was combed neatly and glinted in the light of the candles almost as much as his golden jacket.

"May I have this dance?" he asked with a formal bow.

"You may," I answered with a curtsy.

A shiver stole through me the moment his hand closed

over mine. He swept me up into a graceful dance that made my stomach swirl.

"You steal my breath with your beauty," he said softly.

"And you," I said, smoothing my hand over his shoulder. "A benefit of your occupation."

He grinned widely.

"It is indeed." His gaze swept over me again, lingering on my throat. "Where did you find such a dress? I don't think you'll escape a single man's notice in this."

"If I tell, then everyone will request the same dress. I'll keep the secret of its creation to myself."

He chuckled and pulled me a little closer. Still within propriety's bounds but close enough that I flushed. We danced in silence until the song ended.

"If you haven't yet presented yourself to the King, allow me to escort you." He offered his arm.

"I would rather not. I like the mystery of the mask as my family does not know I'm here. I've been strongly opposed to attending and would prefer to keep my presence a secret."

"Fear not. You are allowed to keep your mystery. It's a simple curtsy with no words exchanged."

I took his arm.

"Perhaps later. First, I need some refreshment."

As he led me from the floor, people parted way for him. I couldn't help but laugh lightly.

"What amuses you?" Kaven asked.

"The way people find value in the quality of your

clothes. Do you think if they met you as I had, they would show the same deference?"

He studied those around us.

"Most assuredly not."

He glanced at me, his gaze warming.

"And that is precisely why I will not allow you to slip from my sight tonight."

"I don't understand."

"They do not only make way for me, princess."

My startled gaze swept the crowd again, and I saw he was correct. Many watched me just as closely as they watched Kaven. What a pair of imposters we were.

Leaving the ballroom, we found the adjoining room set with several long tables groaning under the weight of food the likes of which I'd never seen. People spoke in groups, sipping from flutes of wine or nibbling on tasty tidbits.

"What would you care to sample?" Kaven asked.

"That is an impossible decision. Everything looks delicious."

"Indeed."

The low rumble of his voice sent a wave of heat through me. When I looked up, I found his gaze on my lips.

"Focus," I said softly.

"I've never been more focused."

"On the food."

He sighed and looked at the offerings on the table before us. Without hesitation, he picked up a plate and placed a few options on it.

"Try these."

While I sampled the food, he led me around the room and pointed out the people he knew.

"That is Lord Greylin and his wife. Best to avoid her unless you want to spend the whole evening listening to the merits of their eldest daughter who is a year or two younger than you, I believe."

I chuckled as we moved throughout the room. He knew so much about the people of the court, and I tried to imagine what his life had been like in the shadow of the Prince. Had these people ever given Kaven the consideration he was due for being the intelligent man he was? Probably not. Like Maeve, they probably saw him as a tool. An instrument to be used to find a way into the Prince's inner circle. If the prince even had one.

When I finished my drink and food, Kaven surrendered the dishes to a passing servant and once again swept me onto the dance floor. While we danced, I watched for the Prince and Cecilia, determined to prevent her from cracking his amulet. But there wasn't any sign of either as Kaven and I remained for countless songs, reveling in each other's presence.

Though I enjoyed each moment I spent in his arms, I knew I could not stay there forever. Yet, the passage of time held no meaning until the large clock in the ballroom chimed the eleventh hour. The steady count of eleven rings reminded me of the bird's tapping.

"What has you frowning so?" Kaven asked.

"The hour. I didn't realize how late it had become."

He smiled slightly.

"I will take that as a compliment."

"Where is the Prince?" I asked. "The invitation we received said he was looking forward to seeing me. I should—"

"I'm sure he's occupied with some other maiden. There's no need for you to seek him out."

"You sound jealous."

"When have you ever sought me?" he asked, his gaze serious.

He *was* jealous. Yet, I could do nothing to assure him he had no need to feel so. The knowledge of what yet must be done broke my heart.

"To seek you out would only cause you anguish," I said.

"An anguish I would willingly endure for you."

CHAPTER NINE

I WRENCHED AWAY FROM KAVEN'S HOLD, LEAVING HIM IN THE middle of a dance. He had no idea of what he spoke, for when I sought him out to offer myself to him, I would just as quickly leave him to find the prince.

"Wait," Kaven called.

The crowd parted for me, making my escape from the dance easier. However, it also made it easier for Kaven to catch me by the arm. As he did so, I caught a familiar glimpse of dark hair. I quickly turned away from Porcia to face Kaven.

"Please do not make a scene," I said quietly.

"I wasn't the one to leave my partner in the middle of a dance."

He placed my hand on his arm and escorted me from the room.

"I'll take you to the Royal court where the King is receiving his guests. I'm sure you're likely to see the princely person you so desire there."

We walked in silence through the long, crowded halls. The abundance of people in attendance astounded me. As did the number of guards present. Many of the halls leading from the main one were blocked by the sword wielding men.

"Is this because of me?" I asked. "The additional men and the women?"

"Yes."

He still sounded annoyed.

"I'm sorry."

"Don't be. You were right. Excluding those of common background wasn't likely to keep the Royal family safer. Instead, it was building resentment. Opening the doors to all will garner goodwill."

"And the guards. Will they be able to keep the King and his son safe?"

"No one is safe when there is a caster using magic in secret to cause harm to the kingdom. We have all suffered in some way and will continue to do so until we have her in irons."

"Her?"

He flashed a smile at me.

"Though there have been male casters, the strongest have always been women. One caster, a woman, claimed it was because your gender is more closely tied to the moon and nature."

"Do you believe her?"

He shrugged.

"I've seen the way the woods come alive when you're walking. Who am I to deny there is a connection?"

"But I don't have magic."

"I would argue that you do."

"And that would likely see me hanged or in irons. Hold your infatuated tongue."

He laughed, drawing the attention of the nearby guests. Thankfully, he veered to lead us through two vast and ornately carved doors and out of their view. Concern regarding what might have been overheard faded as I saw what lay ahead.

At the other end of the grand room, a raised dais made it possible for all present to see the King in his splendor, and for our sovereign to view all who attended him. And there were many. The back half of the room was filled with people who watched the proceedings in the front half.

A row of guards stood at the base of the dais, facing the gathering. Before them, a beautifully gowned maiden stepped forward from a short line of girls and curtsied to the King. He nodded, a man to his right welcomed the girl to the ball, and the girl moved to join another far longer line near a side door that was open to the night air.

There, the Prince danced with a pretty maid not

dressed as finely as the others, but based on the glow tinting her cheeks, just as pleased to be in his presence. Not far away from the pair, a small set of musicians played a lovely melody.

While the maid looked entranced, the Prince looked bored.

"He looks less than pleased with his current partner," I said.

"He would rather not have to dance at all," Kaven said with a chuckle, guiding me to the line before the King. "I will meet you at the back of the room after your curtsy." He left my side then, and I felt a stab of guilt at his assumption I would forgo the dance with the Prince.

Glancing back at his retreating form, I caught sight of a woman watching me closely from within the depths of the crowd near the entrance. Her dark eyes swept over me, and I forced myself to calmly turn around and face the King. Although much of her face was hidden by an elaborate mask, I recognized Maeve's dress easily enough. If she was here, Cecilia couldn't be far away.

I surveyed the long line of maids waiting to dance with the Prince and saw Cecilia near the front. I would need to watch her closely. If she managed to crack the amulet, I would need to find a way to warn the Prince before she had a chance to cast a spell.

The line shuffled forward until there was no one else before me. I advanced toward the King and performed a curtsy that would have made my mother proud.

The King's voice rang out, creating a startled hush in the room.

"Rise and let me look at you."

I straightened, heart hammering in fear, and met the King's gaze. If he recognized me, all would be at risk. The urge to look at Cecilia almost overwhelmed me. However, one did not look away from the King. I withstood his scrutiny with as much courage as I possessed until his gaze swept the rest of the room, landing on the Prince approaching to my right.

His grey eyes lit with recognition behind his golden mask.

"Your beauty has silenced the room," he said with a deep bow. "Will you honor me with a dance?"

I looked to the King, who nodded before his gaze swept the room again. Facing the Prince, I accepted the hand he extended and let him sweep me into an extravagant dance that moved so quickly the skirts of my gown flared out. The purpose behind the dance was clear when he pulled me against his chest to steady me.

In my peripheral, I caught sight of Kaven moving through the crowd.

"You are bold," I said softly.

"I am allowed."

"Hardly."

With each turn he brought us closer to the guarded balcony until we danced on the terrace. The doors closed behind us, cutting off the music. He stopped abruptly and grinned at me.

"He will want my head for stealing you away. But can he blame me? I'm awestruck by what a decent dress can do for a maiden's appearance. You are a breathtaking sight," he said. "I can see why Kaven fancies you so."

I pulled myself from his arms and scowled.

"You are purposely provoking him?"

"Never. It is my duty to dance with every maid set before me."

"I wasn't set before you."

"Are you saying you didn't want to dance with me?"

The ass had me cornered. If I denied it, he would send me away and face Cecilia yet this eve. If I acknowledged my desire to dance with him, I would be painted a tease in both the Prince's and Kaven's eyes.

"As we've already danced, there is no point in answering that," I said.

He chuckled.

"Kaven warned me that you are prickly."

"Prickly?" I repeated, offended.

The Prince's grin widened, and I knew then that he was baiting me.

"Must you toy with everyone? You claim Kaven as a friend and disrespect his feelings. You claim to care about your kingdom's welfare but can't be bothered to bestow a kind smile to the maiden before me. Was the cut of her cloth not to your standards?" I demanded, flicking the golden cravat tied at his neck.

"You lecture me not to judge others based on their appearance, yet you do the same."

I opened my mouth to hotly deny his words, and he laughed.

"You truly do not see it? Here I stand, a man you've met thrice, a man you barely know. Based on what action do you believe me to be shallow enough to value a person on their dress?"

"Based on your own words. You just told me my dress made me more appealing."

His smile vanished.

"I've been taught from an early age to play a game. I was told it would keep me safe. My remark on your gown was nothing more than a compliment. My distance from my previous partner was nothing more than an attempt to protect her. There is an evil lurking in this kingdom, and it means to have the throne. Everything I do and say is to prevent that from happening, even bruising the feelings of my closest friend."

We stared at each other for a long moment, and I realized we were more alike than I could have ever imagined.

"Why did you bring me out here, then?"

"Curiosity. I wanted to know if you were the same type of woman as your mother. The type to give up her life to save a kingdom."

"And?"

"I rather hope you are not. I believe life would be dull without you in it." He gestured to the garden. "Would you care to walk?"

I nodded and set my hand on his arm to steady myself as we descended to the well-kept grounds. The scent of honeysuckle teased my nose.

"The gardens are beautiful," I said. "Do you find time to enjoy them?"

"Rarely. Duty has kept me away far too long. And now that I'm here, duty consumes my time. Tell me about yourself."

"What would you like to know?"

"What brings you joy? Sorrow? Anger?"

I breathed deeply, considering his questions. The spell would prevent me from speaking the full truth, but I was determined to speak what truth I could.

"Very little has brought me joy since my mother's death."

"What brought you joy before her death?"

I thought back and smiled.

"Going to town with my sister and stirring up trouble. Reading. My father's returns because he always managed to bring the most marvelous gifts. Walking in the woods. However, losing those I love has brought a sorrow so deep it hurts to breathe at times. There are days it's difficult to remember what once brought me joy. Mostly, I feel anger."

He didn't ask why but walked beside me in silence through the maze of shrubs for a time.

"What brings you joy?" I asked.

"Being home. Seeing my father."

"And sorrow?"

He glanced at me.

"Those I've lost."

I recalled the wife who had looked so much like me and nodded in understanding.

"And anger?"

"The lies and games that are a part of my life every day." The words were laced with the emotion of which he spoke.

I stopped walking and put my hand upon his arm.

"I'm sorry for judging you so harshly. That day in the dungeon..."

"It was an unfortunate way to meet. I had no choice but to question you to the degree that I did. I had to ensure the kingdom's safety. After all, a pretty face does not mean innocence."

"No, it does not." I thought of the women in my home as I agreed with his assessment.

"Will you dine with me tomorrow evening?" he asked suddenly.

"You honor me with the invitation—"

"Speak freely," he said. "Tell me your true thoughts of dining with me."

"My stepmother will not permit it without her as a chaperone."

He smiled.

"That's to be expected. But what are your thoughts? Do you want to dine with me?"

I smiled, my heart aching.

"I do."

He exhaled slowly in return and looked at the castle.

"The hour grows late. I should return you to the court before the ball ends."

"When does it end?"

"At the stroke of midnight. Father insisted, saying that only in silence can he sleep."

Again I thought of the bird's twelve taps.

"I cannot return. Is there a side gate by which I can leave?" I asked, looking around.

"I assure you that Kaven will not be angry that you spent time with me. There is no need to run." His eyes twinkled with amusement.

"I do not seek to avoid Kaven but my family. I begged my stepmother to not force my attendance. She doesn't know I'm here."

His grey eyes studied me for a long moment through the mask.

"Do you think she would disapprove of the time you spent with me?"

"No. She would heartily approve, but she would want to know who I danced with before you."

"Ah. You do not want to admit you danced with Kaven."

"She's made her opposition to him clear," I said.

"I see." He veered to the left. "There is a gate just here. I will only allow you to slip away if you promise to attend the next ball."

"I cannot make such a promise. But I swear I will try to attend."

He smiled, kissed the back of my hand, and nodded to the guard to open the gate for me.

As soon as I was free from the garden, I lifted my skirts and ran. Thankfully, the streets were empty, the majority of Towdown's populace either abed or at the ball. I had made it a fair distance when the castle's clock sounded the first strike of the twelfth hour. My dress began to shimmer. I looked down in astonishment at the outline of my legs through the material.

"No," I groaned, understanding what was happening. The magic was fading.

I ran faster, weaving through streets in my desperation to reach the outskirts of town. I'd barely made it when the final bell rang and the last wisps of magic that made up my dress, shoes, and mask disappeared to leave me in my underclothes.

Whatever magic the tree had used to allow me to escape the estate seemed to hold though because I felt no illness.

Ducking into the woods, I continued on, grateful I

hadn't stripped bare to wear the gown. As I moved, I plucked at my hair, removing the birds' work.

A warm tingle ran under my skin and faded the moment I crossed over the boundary of the estate's land, and I knew the spell allowing me to leave had been spent. I thought of the Prince's invitation and knew the tree's magic hadn't been wasted.

The house was quiet with a candle burning in the window near the door. Knowing I didn't have much time before Maeve returned, I circled the house, retrieved my clothes, then snuck inside.

I'd only just locked myself back in the attic when I heard the carriage roll into the yard. I hurried to wash my muddied feet then sat in the chair by the top of the stairs so I could hear what Cecilia and Porcia had to say as they undressed.

The horses nickered outside, and the carriage moved again. However, the house remained quiet. Without warning, the door to the attic opened. Surprise drove me to my feet and gave Maeve pause.

"You're awake," she said. With a lit candle guiding her, she climbed the steps and looked around the open space suspiciously.

"Why are you still awake, Eloise?"

My mind raced, and I almost smiled as I found the perfect reason.

"I went to sleep during the last ball. You woke me and

said you expected me awake and waiting after the next one."

"You remembered when I did not."

I faked my confusion.

"If you are not here for my attendance, why did you come? Not that I ever mind your attention."

"It's no longer important. As long as you're awake, come downstairs with me."

I followed her to the sitting room where Cecilia paced and Porcia sat, watching her sister warily.

"We must find out who she is," Cecilia said as soon as we entered.

"Calm yourself," Maeve said, blowing out the candle. It wasn't needed in the sitting room. Not only were the lamps lit, but the glow of the fire was strong enough to see the heavy makeup coating Maeve's face. She noticed my stare.

"A necessary measure," she said. "While I wash, Cecilia and Porcia will tell you what happened."

She left the room as I sat beside Porcia. She studied me closely then looked at Cecilia.

"I'm not sure who she is. But she danced with only two men in the main ballroom. First, some boy with a homespun coat and self-made mask, then with a man as devastatingly handsome as the Prince."

"Why are you concerned with this girl?" I asked.

"She captured the Prince's interest so thoroughly that he did not dance with another maiden." At my lack of reaction, she stomped her foot. "He did not dance with me, Eloise. I stood in that line for hours because he allowed the common trash in an hour before the ball was due to start. Hours wasted. When the King asked to look upon her, I wish she would have removed her mask so we might know her face."

Cecilia ripped her own mask from her face and crossed the room to throw it in the fire.

"The Prince and the King weren't the only ones infatuated with her," Porcia said softly. "Every man there watched her."

"Perhaps it was the mystery of her identity," I said.

Cecilia made a derisive sound.

"We were all wearing masks, Eloise. The rest of us didn't garner the same attention as she did."

"Describe her to me," I said. "Was she fair or dark? Did any features that you could see stand out to you?"

"Yes," she said brightening. "You know the people here."

"Not well," I said quickly. "Mother kept us to the estate unless escorted by—"

I couldn't say the names of those now dead.

"It matters not if you know the girl," Maeve said as she re-entered the room. "We will find her and remove her. There is time until the next ball. And since Cecilia never danced with the Prince, there's no need for you to pretend you were there." She sat beside me with a weary sigh. "It's a pity we no longer have my mirror. We would already know the face of our adversary."

"I'm so sorry, Mama," I said quickly.

She patted my hand.

"I do not hold you to blame."

Cecilia flinched and averted her gaze.

"We've all had a long night. It's time for us to retire." She turned to look at me. "Send Heather and Catherine to us. They can assist...with our dresses."

I stood and nodded, not fooled for a moment as to her true intentions.

CHAPTER TEN

Dressed for the day, I went to sit at my table but paused at the sight of the open attic door. I listened, but the house was quiet. I cautiously descended, wondering what Maeve's new game might be. Did she simply expect me to prepare breakfast now that she no longer had servants to do so? Trying not to think of the fate of the maids, I made my way to the kitchen. When I entered the room, I froze in shock at the sight of Catherine and Heather preparing the morning meal.

Staring at the pair, I tried to see if Maeve had done something to them.

"Good morning, miss," Catherine said in a chipper voice.

"We'll have your breakfast ready in just a moment," Heather added. "If you would like to sit in the dining room, I'll bring your morning tea straight away."

I turned and left the kitchen without acknowledging them. I met Maeve as she was just entering the dining room.

"Good. I'm glad you're joining us again," she said.

"As am I. Why, though?"

"You said boredom and seclusion were robbing you of your social skills. That is not something I can allow. You're needed."

Cecilia entered just then.

"Needed for what, Mama?" she asked sharply.

Maeve turned her head slowly, cowing her daughter with a single, cold look.

"Do not mistake your place."

"I'm sorry, Mama." Cecilia sat quickly. Though she tried to appear contrite, the flush of anger stealing into her cheeks, along with her tight jaw, contradicted her effort.

Porcia entered the room last while tying off the end of her braid.

"Good morning, Mama," she said, taking the seat beside Cecilia.

The normalcy of the scene cut me deeply. How dim was the memory of the days when Kellen sat across from me at the table in the kitchen? Of her serious face as I caused some sort of mischief? I hadn't forgotten her, but neither had I thought of her in far too long.

The dining room door swung open, and Catherine entered with a tea set while Heather followed with a tray laden with bowls. They served us quickly and quietly but with good cheer.

"Thank you," Maeve said. "I will call if we need anything else." She waited until they withdrew before addressing us.

"We have one more chance. One more ball in which to impress the Prince. How do you plan to ensure he will choose you as his bride?" She pointedly looked at Cecilia.

"I will not wait for the ball. Each day, from now until the ball, I will invent reasons to go to the estate."

"That is bold and dangerous," Maeve said.

"And we are running out of time."

"The reasons need to be infallible."

"The patch of briarberries is on his land. I will take a basket today to collect anything that remains. When I'm done, I will go to his kitchen to offer them a portion, which is only right now that they are in residence and the bounty is from his land."

"Good." Maeve looked at Porcia next. "How do you plan to ensure he will choose you as his bride?"

Porcia's eyes widened in surprise, and she looked at Cecilia.

"The time for putting all our dreams on only one of you is past," Maeve said coldly. "Do not look at Cecilia to prevent our plans from falling to ruin. What do you plan to do to keep that from happening?"

"I will—"

The dining room door opened.

"Excuse me, mistress. A man just delivered this to me while I was outside."

She handed a letter to Maeve and quickly withdrew.

Maeve broke the King's seal. As she read the note, a smile spread.

"It would seem fortune agrees with Cecilia's plan to find reason to visit the Prince in his home. We've been invited to dinner again."

Porcia visibly sagged in relief.

NERVES TWISTED my stomach as the carriage bumped along the short expanse of road to the Royal Retreat. Surely the Prince would remember that my family knew nothing of my attendance at the ball and would stay silent about the matter. If not, I would have greater concerns than that of Maeve's desire to use me to lure the Prince if Cecilia failed tonight.

I stared out the window, my thoughts in a tangle along with my nerves. There was no escape for me. If Cecilia did succeed in gaining the Prince's interest tonight, I would still need to prevent the marriage from happening by forcing his attentions to me. There was a vast difference between throwing myself at the Prince of my own volition or under Maeve's command, though. Once Maeve committed to using me in full, I felt certain she would cast further spells to control me. My freedoms to thwart her were already far too limited, and I refused to become more of a puppet.

The carriage rolled to a stop, and the door opened. Kaven, backlit and larger than life, waited for us. My heart gave a painful beat at the sight of him.

"Good evening, ladies," he greeted. "His Majesty is waiting for you."

As I was the last to enter, he walked beside me. He didn't speak, but I felt his gaze on me. When I glanced up at him, there was no playful wink. Instead, a look filled with yearning stole my breath.

"I'm delighted you were able to join me tonight," the Prince said the moment we entered his sitting room. Once again, he struck a practiced pose by the fireplace. Though I liked him a little better after our conversation the night before, he still annoyed me.

We curtsied and waited for his invitation to sit in his presence. As soon as we did, Kaven left to fetch our drinks.

The Prince caught my gaze and grinned slightly. Panic laced its way up my throat, constricting my ability to breathe.

"I must say," he said, looking at Cecilia then Porcia, "I was very disappointed not to see any of you at last night's dance."

"We were there, Your Majesty." Cecilia graced him with a beatific smile. "I was standing in line to dance with you. Unfortunately, another swept you away for the rest of the evening. I can't say I recognized her. Who was she?"

"A maiden of mystery, it would seem," he said. "Hopefully, we can all learn more about her at the next ball."

"You wish to see her again?" I asked. "Why?"

"She intrigued me."

"In what way?"

He smiled slightly.

"Her need for mystery."

I wanted to kick him.

"That's no basis for true interest, only mild curiosity."

"Surely you didn't invite us here to speak of another woman," Cecilia said.

He turned toward her and gave an acknowledging bow.

"I assuredly did not. While the balls are my father's idea of a social gathering, I find they leave little room for conversation, which I crave."

After Kaven returned with our drinks, I sipped mine while listening to Cecilia deftly guide the conversation between her and the Prince. Whenever he politely tried to include Porcia or me, she answered on our behalves with a laugh. I glanced at Maeve, who watched it all with an impassivity I knew belied what she truly felt.

"Dinner awaits your command," Kaven said when Cecilia paused to breathe.

"Very good. Will you escort Mistress Cartwright while I escort Porcia?"

Kaven gave a bow and went to Maeve to offer his arm. If she didn't like it, she gave no hint. With a polite smile, she took his arm and let him lead her from the dining room, following Porcia and the Prince. Cecilia looked positively livid as she glared after her sister.

"Why her?" she hissed at me.

"He's being polite and rotating who he escorts," I said. "Or perhaps he noted the way you were cutting everyone else out of the conversation."

She turned her glare on me, and I shrugged.

"If you would rather I tell you idle puffery to the truth, I will gladly do so. You only need to state your preference."

She took a calming breath, smoothed her skirt, and gestured toward the dining room.

"Come, sister. Let us escort one another."

As I walked beside her, I noted her tight jaw and flushed neck. As with Maeve, I walked a fine line with Cecilia. If Maeve didn't decide to openly pit us against one another, I hoped that playing Cecilia's supporter would keep her from targeting me as her competition.

Kaven held out a chair for me beside Maeve's, and another servant helped Cecilia with hers. She seemed mollified by the seating arrangement which placed her to the Prince's right and Maeve to the Prince's left.

"Porcia mentioned there was quite a crush in the main ballroom last night," Cecilia said as the first course was served. "Barely enough room to move. Isn't that right, sister?"

Porcia quickly recovered from her surprise.

"That's right. The number in attendance was

astounding. People were making use of your gardens to escape the crowd and provide more room for the dancers."

"Were you able to find suitable partners among the masked throng?" the Prince asked her, making me bristle.

"Yes, Your Majesty. A mask cannot hide one's wealth or standing with the Crown."

His gaze shifted to me, a hint of knowing amusement glinting in the depths of his eyes.

"And what did you think of the ball?" he asked.

My heart gave a violent lurch.

"I did not attend, Your Highness."

He frowned.

"Did you not receive my invitation specifically requesting your presence?"

"We did, Your Grace," Maeve said smoothly. "While we regret Eloise's absence last eve, we hope she will be able to attend the final ball."

He nodded to Maeve and set his soup aside only half eaten. Kaven quickly removed the dish. I wondered if the Prince's attitude frustrated Kaven as much as it did me.

"Will there be a theme for the final ball?" Cecilia asked, seizing the lull in conversation.

"I hadn't yet considered one. Do you have suggestions?"

"Something more intimate would give you an opportunity for conversation such as this," she said. "Perhaps a ball where attendees must offer a gold coin tribute to the Crown. The coins collected could then be used to improve the lives of those unable to attend."

I wondered if she could even hear herself. The servants cleared the rest of the first course and prepared for the next as the Prince answered.

"A kind gesture."

If he truly thought so, then I had never met two people more matched. If not for Cecilia's tendency to destroy, maim, and kill, I would leave the Prince to her greedy aspirations.

"While I appreciate the prospect of a smaller crowd, limiting our guest list, now, would only cause ill will among the people of Towdown and the Kingdom of Drisdall. I fear my need for quiet conversation will need to wait until I'm wed."

"Or until you invite us to dine with you again," Porcia said.

He chuckled.

"Indeed."

"Perhaps a color-themed ball, then. The ladies could dress in red and the men in royal blue."

"A fascinating idea. However, I did enjoy the mystery of the masks."

Cecilia's smile became a bit more brittle.

"And I wouldn't have this ball become a financial burden on anyone but my father," he said. "With so many already having masks, it seems the wisest choice. Plus, there is a certain level of equality when those with a less discerning eye cannot gauge the social standing of their partner."

For a moment, the conversation came to a halt.

"Eloise told us of your lovely trophy room, Your Majesty," Maeve said, breaking the uncomfortable silence. "Perhaps, when you're finished, you would be so kind as to show it to Cecilia."

He looked at Cecilia.

"Dead things interest you?"

I almost choked on my mouthful of tender meat.

"What interests you, interests me, Your Grace," Cecilia said skillfully.

"Then I would be delighted to escort you. But only if Eloise and Kaven follow us as chaperones."

Cecilia glanced at me, her smile never faltering. But, I could see the resentment because I was once again being included.

I nodded my agreement, only after Maeve gave her consent. When I glanced at Kaven, he watched me intently, not even trying to hide the attention he bestowed me. Shifting my gaze to my plate, I took another bite. I needed to remain focused on the Prince and Cecilia, not the memory of the time I'd spent dancing within Kaven's embrace. Yet, that was exactly where my mind dwelled. I recalled each touch and each look until my skin heated. Surely, he wouldn't say or do anything in Cecilia's presence that would give away our time together.

Too nervous to eat more, I set my fork aside, a signal that I was finished. As if the Prince had been waiting for me, he put his aside as well then stood.

"Shall we?" he asked, offering his arm to Cecilia.

Something brushed against my right arm, and I looked up to find Kaven standing beside me.

"Miss Cartwright?" he said formally.

I placed my hand in his and stood. His fingers caressed my skin as he set my hand on his arm. Steeling myself against Kaven, I looked at Maeve who watched us closely. This time, I was far too wise to show any preference for Kaven.

Giving her a small nod, I focused on Cecilia and the Prince as they left the room ahead of us. No matter the discomfort caused by the spell binding me to Maeve's proximity, I couldn't let the Prince and Cecilia out of my sight.

Whereas Kaven and I walked with a respectable distance between us, Cecilia leaned toward the Prince, letting his arm brush against her side.

"Do you plan to stay at the Retreat long?" Cecilia asked as they entered the adjoining room.

"Only until a bride is announced," he said. "My father will require us to live at the palace from then until the vows are spoken. After that, there is a tour of the kingdom to present the new princess."

"That sounds lovely," she said. "Will the King tour with the bride and groom?"

"That has not yet been decided." They slowed their pace to walk among the creatures. I was so focused on them that Kaven's abrupt halt made me stumble.

His eyes twinkled with amusement.

"There's no need to follow them further," he said. "We can watch from here."

Even as he said that, the pair disappeared behind the largest bear I'd ever seen. I was about to protest that we needed to follow when I heard Cecilia's next question.

"What is this?" A moment of silence followed. "Please tell me it is not a cameo of your late wife. I cannot hope to win your affection from a ghost."

Those words were spoken with sad acceptance, but I knew better.

Kaven's gaze turned serious, and he led me forward. We rounded the bear to find Cecilia touching the prince's chest, her fingers circling a spot near the end of his cravat.

"It is not a cameo," he said, taking her hand. "And my affections are not held by a ghost of the past."

"Such news relieves me," Cecilia said with a smile. "If not a cameo, what is it? It has an odd shape. Might you show me?"

He chuckled and began loosening his cravat. I didn't think. Instead, I purposely stumbled into Kaven hard enough to send him into the bear. The next few seconds slowed. The Prince glanced at the unstable bear and Kaven. Kaven reached out to prevent the creature's fall. Cecilia, her gaze fixed on the stone barely peeking from the Prince's loosened clothing, clasped a hunting mallet from a nearby display.

Without thought of consequence, I threw myself into

the Prince, sending us both away from the rocking bear. He landed with a grunt, and my forehead connected with his chin as I toppled onto him.

"Forgive me, Your Majesty," I said, already scrambling off.

He blinked up at me with a widening grin as I offered him a hand.

"You continue to surprise me, Eloise. And no forgiveness is needed for such a selfless rescue." He rose to his feet without aid and righted his clothing. I breathed easier when the amulet was safely tucked away once more.

The Prince took my hand and bowed low over it. The feel of his lips on my skin sent a tingle of fear through me. What had I done?

"I will never forget this moment," he said.

He released me and looked over my right shoulder.

"Shall we continue our tour?"

I moved to the side, too afraid to look at Cecilia.

"Of course, Your Grace," she answered smoothly, stepping forward to take his arm once more. "Are you well? The fall didn't hurt you, did it?"

"No. I'm well. Your sister truly acted heroically."

As they moved on, I looked up at Kaven. He studied me carefully.

"What was that all about?" he asked softly.

"A clumsy attempt to right a possible wrong," I said. "My stumble sent you into the bear, and it looked like it might topple onto the Prince."

"And me. Or did you forget I was here."

The words cut deeply.

"I didn't forget. However, the King is less likely to imprison me if injury befalls you. I'm truly sorry, Kaven."

He didn't offer his arm again as he went to follow the Prince and Cecilia. Heart breaking, I followed in Kaven's wake until the couple completed their tour and returned to the dining room.

"Your daughters are lovely," the Prince said with a smile at Maeve. "Would you care for an after-dinner libation before you depart?"

"Please," Cecilia all but purred, not yet relinquishing his arm.

We moved to the sitting room where the Prince gracefully detached Cecilia and went to his favorite place before the fire.

"Mistress Cartwright, I would like the honor of walking Eloise home," he said without preamble.

Maeve's brows rose in shock. My stomach pitched, and I glanced at Cecilia. Cold hatred burned in her eyes. Porcia looked stunned.

"Chaperoned, of course," the Prince assured. "I will have one of my staff follow us."

I looked at Maeve, who watched the Prince closely. That she was pleased with the offer was evident in the ever so slight curving of her lips.

"While I would never deny the Crown Prince anything, as a Mother, I must also protect my daughter. A walk alone after dark is hardly suitable for an unmarried miss, even with a chaperone. I must ask what your intentions are."

"A show of gratitude, only. There was a mishap in the trophy room, and Eloise showed great care for my safety. I wish to repay that care with a few moments of my time. That is all."

"But of course, then," Maeve said. "I will hold you to your promise of a chaperone and trust you won't linger in the woods. It pains me to let my daughters out of my sight. This world can be a terrible place without the protection of a parent."

Understanding lit. Maeve would not free me from my curse for this walk. The moment she left me, I would feel the sickness of separation until I reached the estate's boundary.

Kaven arrived with the tray of drinks.

"Kaven, fetch Mrs. Wallace. I would like her to accompany me when I escort Eloise home."

"Here," Cecilia said standing. "Allow me to serve in your place as the hour grows late."

Kaven reluctantly handed her the tray and left the room. Cecilia served the Prince first, saving the last cup for herself.

"A toast to friendships," Cecilia said, raising her glass. "May ours continue to grow." She stared into the Prince's eyes as she took a sip.

"Indeed," he said, lifting the cup to his lips.

While Cecilia guided the conversation, I drank deeply

of the sweet wine in hopes it would help dull the sickness to come. A pleasant numbness spread throughout my body before I emptied the glass.

An elderly woman entered the room. Her white hair was piled on top of her head in a long braid and a cloak was pulled over her shoulders. A pang of guilt struck me as her eyes swept the room. Walking through the woods was probably the last thing she wanted to do this evening.

"Ah, Mrs. Wallace," the Prince said. "Thank you for joining us."

"Of course, Your Majesty."

He drank the remainder of his wine and set the cup to the side.

"Come girls," Maeve said, standing. She curtsied to the Prince. "I will await my daughter at home."

He nodded and turned to me as Maeve and the others left the room.

"A few quiet moments at last," he said. He held out his hand to me then cringed. "If you will excuse me for a moment." He hurried from the room, leaving me alone with Mrs. Wallace.

"Hello," I said with a smile I didn't feel. My insides were already starting to twist violently. "I'm Eloise. It's nice to meet you, Mrs. Wallace."

"And you too, dear. The Prince seems quite taken with you."

"I'm nothing more than a curiosity to him."

"Oh? Why do you think that?"

"I'm told my mother once saved the kingdom."

"Indeed, she did. You look like her. Her hair was dark, though, and her skin paler."

"You knew her?"

"I'm old enough to know most people," she said with a smile.

Kaven strode into the room before I could ask her anything further.

"Mrs. Wallace, the Prince requests your presence."

Her brow rose.

"I know. That is why I'm here, silly boy."

Kaven grinned.

"It would seem the Prince's dinner isn't agreeing with him."

"I see." She looked at me. "Excuse me, Miss Eloise. It was a pleasure to meet you."

As soon as she left the room, my insides gave a violent pull.

"I must go," I said. "Please make my excuses."

I hurried to leave the room before I vomited on the floor, but Kaven grabbed my arm as I passed him.

"I can't allow you to walk home alone."

CHAPTER ELEVEN

"Is this the leisurely pace you would have set with the Prince?" Kaven asked.

His long legs had no trouble keeping up with me.

"You needn't sound so jealous," I said, too miserable to censor my words. "He is the one who wanted to walk me home. One does not deny the Prince what he wants."

"You're right. Most people wouldn't deny him. You are not most people. If you didn't want to walk with him, you would have refused."

He grabbed my arm again to stop me. My stomach heaved with the need to get to Maeve, and I kicked him in the shin. He yelped as he released me, and I picked up my skirts to run, no longer caring about appearances.

Surely Maeve had to know this would happen. What had she been thinking? The Prince would have been put out if I emptied my stomach in front of him.

Kaven caught up with me the moment I crossed over the estate's boundary and everything eased inside of me. This time, when he grabbed my arm, I stopped.

"Why did you kick me?" he demanded.

"Because you're being a grabby ass," I said, pulling my arm from his. "The Prince asked to walk me home, not lay me on the grass and have his way with me. Unlike you, who has taken uncountable liberties with me, the Prince's behavior has been above reproach. Now tell me truly, would he have done something to me on this walk home?"

"It's not what he might have done but what you might have allowed," Kaven said.

I slapped him hard, the crack ringing through the trees.

"I have never allowed any man what I've allowed you. And I regret—"

Eyes blazing, he gripped my shoulders and kissed me with a fury that left my lips bruised and body aching. After a moment, his hold softened. His hands smoothed down my arms, and I lost myself to the sweep of his tongue against mine.

Kaven was many things to me, but most of all, he was my anchor. The one bit of reality I could trust to be true to me with his feelings and his words. He was angry and hurt because he thought he might be losing me to the Prince. And he was right. I hated everything in that moment. Mostly myself. I didn't want to break Kaven or his dream of a future with me.

I poured the desperation and need I felt into the kiss,

and when he finally pulled away, we were both gasping for air.

"I'm sorry," he whispered.

"Don't," I said, placing my finger over his lips. I needed him. Not just in that moment but in my life in any capacity. I stood on my toes to kiss his chin and jaw. Then, I reclaimed his lips for a bittersweet kiss.

"Will you wait here for me?" I asked softly. "I must return to the house so no one comes looking for me. But will you wait for me to return once everyone is abed?"

"Yes." The word was hoarse and full of need.

I kissed him once more then fled.

Inside the house, candles lit the entry, and the glow of the fire from the sitting room let me know that Maeve waited. However, she wasn't alone. Cecilia paced before the fireplace while Porcia sat nearby. All three looked at me the moment I entered.

"Traitor," Cecilia hissed.

"What were you thinking?" I countered, knowing I walked a dangerous line. "That he would just stand there as you clubbed his amulet? You risked us all with your rashness."

Her eyes widened, and she glanced at Maeve, who stilled.

"What happened?" Maeve asked with deadly calm.

"A small lapse in judgement, Mama," I said. "I'm sure it won't happen again."

Her gaze narrowed and pinned Cecilia.

"You were going to attempt to crack the amulet? While he was wearing it?"

"If it was cracked, we wouldn't need to worry about which of us held his interest," Cecilia said quickly. "I could cast a—"

Maeve stood and stalked toward her daughter. Porcia winced as her mother struck her sister hard. Cecilia didn't make a noise though I knew it had to hurt.

Maeve turned to me.

"Does he suspect?"

"No. I pushed him out of the way under the ruse that I was saving him."

Maeve exhaled slowly.

"And the walk home? Were you able to make any progress toward capturing his interest?"

"Even if he hadn't fallen ill and been unable to walk me, it would have been impossible to do more than run home because of the spell," I said.

Her gaze darkened again.

"Are you reproaching me?"

"No, Mama. I'm explaining the reason behind my failure. I cannot hope to compete with Cecilia or Porcia when it comes to the Prince."

She studied me thoughtfully.

"But only because of the restrictions. He's very drawn to you with little effort from yourself."

I said nothing.

"Tomorrow, you and I will go to town. We will see if

you're worthy of my trust. Perhaps then, you will be a true contender."

Cecilia hid her fisted hands in her skirts as her mother turned to her.

"I find it odd that the Prince fell ill just after we left and was unable to escort your sister as he planned. Do you have anything to say on the matter?"

"I intend for him to wed me."

"I see. And the illness?"

"A simple powder in his drink to loosen his bowels. Nothing magic. Only an undetectable compound of herbs."

"As I said this morning, I care not which of you weds him—only that one of you does. Do not let your jealousy and ambitions prevent us from attaining our goal, Cecilia. When one of you succeeds, we will all be rewarded. There will be no more mistakes from you. You will not improvise. If you find yourself unable to follow my command precisely as it's given, I have no need of you. Do you understand?"

Cecilia's angry flush drained from her face, leaving only a ghostly paleness.

"Yes, Mama."

Maeve looked at the three of us.

"You've taxed me. I will speak with you all again in the morning."

She swept from the room; and Porcia, still seated, looked from Cecilia to me.

"Leave," Cecilia said, and Porcia quickly fled.

Cecilia closed the distance between us. Though I knew she couldn't hurt me physically, she and Maeve had taught me there were worse forms of punishment.

"I will share a bit of advice with you, dear sister. Daughters are easily replaced. Never forget that."

With those ominous words spoken, she left. I waited until her door closed to go to my room. There, I listened at the vents, waiting for the house to settle. My mind whirled with too many thoughts. What would Maeve's test of loyalty entail, and did I want to pass it? If I passed Maeve's test tomorrow, she would surely push me to win the Prince on her behalf. If I didn't pass it, she would still use me to bed the Prince. I was running out of time. Relief coursed through me that I'd asked Kaven to wait.

When I knew everyone slept, I snuck from the house with a quilt under my arm. Fear and nerves for what was to come made me jumpy until I reached the clearing and saw Kaven waiting there. He turned at my approach. Seeing him, his strength, his certainty, helped calm me.

With soft amusement, he watched me spread the quilt on the ground. That amusement faded as I sat and began loosening my gown.

"What are you doing?"

I paused, trying to read him. He'd made his interest and intent quite plain. He wanted me. Was he, like me, ignorant as to how specifically the deed should be done?

"Undressing. I thought it was required for sex. If my skirts don't get in the way, my underthings certainly will."

His gaze heated, following the movement of my fingers as I plucked at the cords for my bodice. He joined me on the quilt and caught my hands in his.

"I want you, Eloise. But not here. Not like this."

I looked at him, trying not to let my frustration show. Neither of us had the luxury of waiting for a ceremony that might never happen. If my fate was to sacrifice myself to the Prince, then who I gave my innocence to would be of my own choosing.

"I don't know my future. I don't know if I can give you what you want. But, this? This I can give. This is my choice. What's yours?"

Anger clouded his eyes.

"There is time. No one else will touch you until we are ready."

"How can you be sure?" I demanded. "You cannot possibly know my mind or anyone else's to foresee the future. How do you know I'm not already promised to another? Maeve alluded as much."

His expression darkened further.

"You are mine."

He gripped the back of my head and brought his lips to mine in a kiss filled with passion, anguish, and need. I held him just as tightly, feeling the same.

This time, it was his fingers tugging at the cords of my clothes as his heated kisses trailed from my mouth to my breasts. He plucked at one peak while he suckled the other. I shivered at the sensation and threaded my fingers through his hair, delighted in the feel of his tongue on my skin as he lowered me to the quilt. A heat began in my breast and spread to my middle. The warmth grew to an ache that pulsed with each suckle of his hot mouth.

His sudden abandonment of my flesh drew a soft mewl of denial from my lips, and I looked up at him.

"You rob me of all thought and blind me to consequence." His palm covered my exposed breast. "I am yours, Eloise. For all time. Tell me you are mine."

"I am yours tonight if you'll have me," I said.

He made an angry sound and dipped his head to claim the other breast. I gasped and arched into his mouth. The rub of his whiskers as he nuzzled me added to the tingle of pleasure, and I held him close, desperate for him to continue.

Something tugged at my skirt a moment before the fingers of his free hand glided up my legs. He suckled harder, distracting me so thoroughly, I didn't at first notice the tug on my underthings.

He lifted his head just as the material loosened.

"Tell me you'll wait for me. Wait for our vows," he said.

"She is set against our union," I said, speaking of Maeve. "My fate may not be my own to promise."

Anger clouded his expression.

"You would wed another after laying with me."

"I would give a piece of myself to you so you would always remember the love I bear for you, no matter what direction life takes me."

"You are the most stubborn—"

Lifting my mouth to his, I silenced his protest with a stroke of my tongue. A growl of frustration reverberated from him. The kiss shifted from my lead to his as he pushed my skirts higher. His fingers tugged harder at my underthings, exposing me to the night air. He broke away, panting. Instead of again questioning my choice, he met my gaze as his fingers brushed over my netherhair. I swallowed hard, trying not to let my fear of the unknown show.

He shifted his weight, nudging my legs open. I gasped and closed my eyes as his fingers feathered lower, parting my folds. A rush of heat swathed me as he gently explored me until he found a spot that sent a rush of pleasure coursing through me. There he stroked over my flesh for several moments.

I panted and spread my legs further to give him better access. He dipped his head to kiss my breast then nibbled his way up my throat. As he did so, his finger strokes dipped lower and lower until he teased my opening.

He brushed his lips over mine then lifted his head to look at me.

"I love you, Eloise," he said softly. Then his finger delved inside of me.

Any discomfort at the invasion quickly melted into pleasure as he slowly retreated and advanced. My legs moved of their own accord, twitching and straightening. A need built inside of me, growing in intensity.

His mouth closed over my breast once again. This time, I felt the scrape of his teeth on my flesh. A tingle jolted from my chest to between my legs, intensifying the pleasure of his fingers. Small sounds escaped me, and I gripped his shoulders.

He pulled away abruptly, leaving me exposed to the night air. I opened my eyes to see him loosening his pants. For one brief, horrible moment, I saw Hugh.

Clenching my eyes closed, I banished the thought. This was Kaven. He was safe. He would carefully take from me what I would entrust to no other.

"Eloise?" Kaven asked softly, his hand cupping my face. "Look at me."

When I opened my eyes again, Kaven was looking down at me with concern.

"It's not too late to change your mind."

"About what? Loving you? Never."

He smiled slightly and kissed me softly. His fingers returned to work their magic and reignited the needful flames that licked at me from inside. My mind emptied of thought as I allowed myself to feel every heated stroke. Every heated kiss. I began arching my hips in time with his touch. His mouth returned to my breast, and the sensation sent me into a spiral of pleasure I'd never thought possible. I cried out as it pulsed through me, clenching around Kaven's hand. He didn't stop moving his fingers until he'd wrung every last bit of wonder from me.

"That is just the beginning," he promised, settling his weight over me. His fingers were replaced with something thicker and warmer.

Dazed, I looked up into his eyes as he eased into me. His shaft stretched me with stinging discomfort.

"Wait," I gasped.

He set his glistening forehead against mine.

"Discomfort will give way to what you've just experienced. I swear to you."

I nodded, and he withdrew only to ease into me once more. It felt less invasive the second time. He didn't press further though I knew he wasn't fully seated. He stroked me, letting me feel the returning pleasure. I rocked up to meet him and a lance of pain pierced me. I cried out sharply, and he muted the sound with a hard kiss.

After a moment, the pain faded and his tongue distracted me. He broke away to kiss my jaw and my eyelids.

"I'm sorry for that," he breathed. "I wasn't expecting you to move."

"I wouldn't have if I'd known it would hurt."

"It won't again. Not like that."

As if to prove his words, he withdrew and slowly entered me once more. It felt odd, but not unpleasant. He reached between us, his fingers finding that spot that sent so much pleasure through me and rocked into me again. Before long, I was gasping and arching into each thrust.

There was no room for his hand between us as his hips met mine again and again with a force that returned me to that moment of anticipation. This time, when the pleasure erupted, I knew what to expect and let myself tumble headlong into it.

Kaven's pace increased before he thrust deeply and stilled. His cock twitched within me, sending echoes of pleasure pulsing through my core. A low groan erupted from him a moment before his lips claimed mine. The kiss was sweet and tender and perfect.

Our breathing calmed, and I relished the feel of him on me even if he was still fully clothed. It was better that way. The image of his body wouldn't haunt me when I lay with the Prince.

"I swear I will not let you go," Kaven said as if hearing my thoughts. "You are mine, now and always."

I tilted my head back and looked up at him, my heart shattering.

"For now, you must," I said lightly. "I need to return before anyone discovers me missing."

He looked about to object. I placed a soft kiss upon his lips to prevent him from saying anything further. The time for words between us was finished. All that remained were actions. And, I knew that no words could amend those once done.

"Fine. I will release you for now. But know that I do not like doing so."

He rolled off of me and watched me stand, his gaze caressing my exposed breasts.

"I will never tire of looking at you," he said.

I tightened my bodice and hurried to leave before my despair showed.

IT HURT TO SIT. I hadn't counted on that when joining Maeve and my stepsisters for breakfast. I hadn't counted on it aching every time I took a step, either. Had I not seen his manhood and known it to be a part of his flesh, I would have questioned what Kaven bludgeoned my insides with the night before.

Was that the way of life, then? No pleasure without pain? No happiness without misery?

A sigh escaped me.

"Is something amiss?" Maeve asked.

"No, Mama. Nothing amiss. Just a pinch of melancholy."

She patted my hand.

"Something easily remedied then. After you complete your task, we can visit the market and shop for whatever you'd like."

Cecilia's eyes stayed fixed on her bowl where she idly stirred her oats.

"Porcia, while we're out, I would like you to go berry

picking and visit the Retreat as Cecilia proposed. Until the Prince chooses, you must all try to capture his attention."

"Yes, Mama," Porcia said.

"As soon as your sister is done playing with her food, we can leave," Maeve said, once again facing me. Cecilia immediately stopped what she was doing.

"I apologize, Mama. My appetite is absent this morning."

"Very well." Maeve stood. "Seth has everything prepared and the carriage waiting for us."

I dutifully followed, keeping any twinges of discomfort from showing on my face. A task that became more difficult during the jostling carriage ride to town. It wasn't until the carriage stopped that I saw we'd almost reached the docks.

Trepidation filled me as I looked out the window. We weren't far from where I'd woken the last time I'd been to town...when I'd walked the streets naked.

The carriage door opened, and Seth was there to offer Maeve a hand.

"Thank you," she said graciously, stepping down. "Remember, a woman in labor is the reason you will give. Nothing more. Keep everyone away."

The trepidation only grew stronger as Maeve led Cecilia and me to a rundown building and opened the door. There was nothing but darkness ahead when we stepped inside. The door shut behind us with a snick.

"Stay where you are."

A moment later, a spark ignited in the abyss, and flames slowly grew.

"Come along." She led us through a barren room that faintly smelled of musty old hay and dirt. A noise came from the doorway ahead.

My steps slowed, and Cecilia, who followed me, nudged me forward.

"Where is your courage, sister?" she asked softly.

"In the carriage. I should probably fetch it."

She snorted and prodded me forward toward Maeve, who stood just inside the room.

When I entered, I immediately saw the cause for the noise. A hooded man was bound to a chair, the only furniture in the room.

Fear coiled in my gut.

"Who is that?" I asked softly.

Maeve walked to him and yanked back the hood. Alfie blinked against the lamp's light.

"Why?" I asked.

"He did recognize you."

His gaze locked onto mine. I could see the terror there.

"He won't say anything," I said.

"I know." Maeve smoothed a hand over his hair. "I've already completed that spell, a mercy to repay him for the kindness he showed you. Much safer than cutting out his tongue."

He swallowed hard and paled. I felt like doing the same

but knew better than to show what I felt. Instead, I met Maeve's gaze.

"Since he was so willing to help you once, I thought he would be the perfect candidate to help me test your loyalty."

"How?" I asked.

"Take his eyes."

CHAPTER TWELVE

HORROR SHOULD HAVE FILLED ME AT HER SUGGESTION. THAT it didn't showed how much I'd already endured. Instead, I felt fear for Alfie. That fear fed the well of my anger.

"You can cut his eyes out with this," Maeve said, withdrawing a knife from her pocket and offering it to me. The lamp's light glinted off the lethal edge of the blade.

Cecilia pushed me toward her.

"Find your courage, sister. He's nothing to you. Do this and ensure your place."

Alfie paled.

"I can't."

Maeve's hand remained outstretched as she considered me.

"Can't means you're physically unable. I see nothing preventing you from doing as I asked. You have full use of your hands. You can hold yourself upright. You can see and move." She sighed. "You can, Eloise. I will tell you again. Cut out his eyes. Now, choose your response wisely."

"I refuse to intentionally harm another."

Maeve lowered the knife.

"I see. But, where was that refusal when you stabbed Hugh in the eye with the poker? I quite liked him. His death was a waste."

"It was. And though, through defense of my person, he was killed by my hand, I do not carry the weight of blame for his death."

She arched a brow at me.

"I see."

"Stupid," Cecilia said softly behind me.

Maeve's necklace began to glow.

"You will learn your place," she said a moment before I sank into the nothingness of oblivion.

I TURNED my head and vomited while still laying down. This time, I didn't wonder what was happening to me. I knew. Maeve had spelled me to sleep then left me. I spat and breathed through my nose, inhaling the same musty smell as before. She hadn't moved me this time.

Did she honestly think another naked walk through town would make me more compliant? There was nothing she could do to me that would ever force my hand enough to cut out—

"'Bout time you're awake," a rough voice said from nearby.

I jerked upright, the movement sending my stomach into another fit. The man laughed as I heaved.

"She said you would be sick and easy to handle."

Fear skittered its way up my spine as I remembered her last promise of punishment to have men hold me down and defile me in ways that would haunt my dreams until my death.

"Nothing I could catch, though," he continued. "She promised me that."

Fingers tangled into my hair and wrenched me upright.

"Let's have a look at you."

Anchored in place by my hair, I couldn't escape his other hand, which gripped my chin.

"You're a beauty. Ain't no dirt ever going to hide that."

Trying to focus, I blinked against the dim light of the lamp. The craggy face of an almost bald man swam into view. Yellow teeth gleamed as he grinned at me. His gaze swept over my face then lower. He made a satisfied sound.

"Ain't seen flesh so firm in far too many years."

He released my chin and covered one breast with his hand. Weakly, I smacked his touch away. He laughed.

"You're a mite thing. Barely any meat to you and no fight. Not worth my time, really."

My panic hitched higher. I struggled to push back the sickness enough to focus on protecting myself. Placing my hand in the middle of his stained shirt, I pushed with all my might.

He laughed again.

"You have more fight than I thought. Best we get this done then. She paid me well."

He released my hair, and I collapsed to the ground once more, my hand landing in my own upheaval. I gagged and tried to move away. The man's hand closed around my bare hip.

"None of that now."

I kicked out at him. His chuckle echoed in the room as he caught my ankle and pulled on my leg, dragging me.

"What a fine sight your cunny is. Are you pure? I ain't ever bedded one still with her maidenhead. In my youth, I didn't want the fumbling or crying. Just a good, wet fuck. Virgins never give you that. At least, that's what my pa told me."

All the while he spoke, he tugged me across the floor, bit by bit. I clawed at the dirt, trying to dig in and stop him. But I couldn't. I tried kicking and jerking my leg from his firm grip, but nothing worked.

"Here we are," he said. "I can't stand while I do this anymore. My knees can hold a fierce grudge. You hold still while I get ready."

He released me, and I rolled myself to my belly before hefting my weight up. The room swam dizzily. Nearby, I spotted a chair. One of the back rails was missing, and blood smeared the seat. Swallowing thickly, I turned my head away and saw the old man. He picked up something from a small table and turned toward me. The knife glinted in the light.

"No," I said, shuffling back.

"The time for fighting is past. Sit still and let me have my way with you."

He grabbed my hair and sat in the chair, yanking me toward his crotch. The odor of sweat and feces clogged my nose. I closed my eyes, sobbing silently, and struggled to pull away. He held firm. A weird noise almost escaped my notice in my efforts to free myself, but the feather soft tickle on my arm had me turning my head and opening my eyes.

"Be still," he said with another tug.

I blinked at the golden thread on my bicep, trying to understand its significance as that same odd noise repeated itself. My gut clenched, and the need to gag almost overwhelmed me as a hank of my hair drifted to the ground before my eyes. He sliced thrice more before I realized what he was doing. I began my struggles anew.

"I almost nicked you, twit. Stop moving, or you'll be as bloody as the boy that were here."

His words stilled me. I cared nothing about my own bleeding but that of Alfie.

"They killed him?" I slurred.

"Ain't my place to say."

With a vengeance, he went at my hair. Too grief-numb to fight, I stayed still between his legs.

"There now. You're done. Off you go. She told me to tell you she's waiting."

He grasped me under my arms and hefted me to my feet, taking the opportunity to paw at my breasts again. I swatted away from his hold and, ignoring his chuckle, stumbled toward the door.

The sunlight nearly blinded me when I stepped outside. The sound of water and the smell of salt cleansed the scent of the old man from my nose. I breathed in deeply, fighting the sickness trying to consume me. The pull to return to Maeve drove me to move.

"Who-who!" a man yelled. "A fine piece of ass if I've ever seen one. I'll give you four copper to suck my cock."

I didn't turn to look but shuffled forward.

"Don't be like that," the same voice yelled.

"I'll give you a half silver if you let me stick my cock anywhere I want," another voice called. Raucous laughter followed.

I stopped moving and turned toward the ships where men were lined up on the decks.

"I have the pox," I yelled, trying not to heave, "and a rash that burns fiercely each time my bowels let loose, which is far too often for my comfort. I have no coin to see a doctor, but if I suck all of your cocks, surely, I'll earn enough. When I'm cured, my cunny will be open for business again."

Several of the men made faces and turned away without a word. Those who still lingered no longer smiled.

"Come now," I cajoled. "My mouth is clean." My stomach chose that moment to revolt, and I heaved into the dirt.

"Get gone, wretch!" one of the men yelled.

I smiled and turned away from their accusatory gazes. How often men only praised external beauty when they thought they could benefit from it. Shallow creatures. No worse than women, though, I supposed. My sex judged just as harshly with their gossip.

A lump of cloth huddled near the next building slowed my steps. Something about it seemed familiar. Placing my hand on the wall for support, I blinked at the trousers. I'd seen them before. Hadn't I?

The soft sound of sobbing reached my ears.

"Are you all right?" I managed to ask.

The lump cringed then straightened, turning his head toward me. A bloody bandage covered his eyes, but I still recognized Alfie.

"Leave me, I beg you. Pay me no kindness."

My stomach heaved again, but there was nothing left in me. When I looked up, I caught sight of Cecilia standing at the end of the lane. She watched me with a twisted smile.

"I will show you no kindness today," I said softly. "But soon."

He started sobbing again and leaned his head against the wall.

Straightening away, I started forward once more. Once I was past the boy, Cecilia disappeared from sight. I followed the pull from the dock and through several narrow streets before it began to ease. At the next corner, I turned and the sickness vanished completely. The carriage waited only a few steps away, along with five buckets of water and Cecilia with a cloth and my dress.

"Hello, sister," she said with a twisted smile.

"Hello." I picked up a bucket and poured it over my head then rinsed my mouth from the second one before dumping that over me as well. When I reached for the cloth, she pulled it away.

"All of them. I pulled them from the well, just now, for you."

I emptied them in quick succession as she watched me.

"Your act of defiance changed nothing," she said. "The boy still lost his sight but by my hand. When will you learn and start listening to Mama."

Without answering, I took the cloth from her hand and rubbed it over my face and head.

"Your hair is quite lovely, sister."

"Thank you. I will be sure to refer you to the barber."

She shook her head, tossed my dress at me, and opened the carriage door.

I got in naked and tugged the dress on as Maeve watched.

"Based on your impertinent answers, I can see you have learned nothing."

"But I have, Mama."

"And what is that?" she asked.

"Cecilia is just like you."

LOCKED AWAY IN THE ATTIC, I cleaned myself as best as I could, using the washbasins Porcia had filled. I was grateful they were continuing to keep the staff safe from my vile influence. After today, I didn't think I could bear to witness anyone else's suffering. As it was, my anger had loosened my tongue far too much in front of Cecilia and Maeve.

I studied my reflection in the mirror and ran my hand over my coarsely cropped hair. Too short to lay flat, it stuck out in any direction it saw fit. Losing my hair angered me but not out of some misguided vanity. How would I now attend the ball without being recognized? And if I couldn't attend, how would I stop Maeve from getting everything she wanted?

Turning from the mirror, I dressed and went to the window. Birds flitted about in the branches, their merry songs barely reaching my ears. I wished to walk among the trees. To feel the sun on my face. To forget the bloody blindfold covering Alfie's eyes. Most of all, I wanted to cry. But, I refused to do it here where someone might witness my sorrow. Instead of doing any of that, I stared at the woods I loved and lost hours to memories of better times.

The door opened, pulling me from my reverie. When I turned, my knees ached, and I thought of the old man with a shudder. It could have been worse. He could have tried to use me. Never had I been more glad to have given myself to Kaven than the moment I heard the man compliment my firm flesh.

Footsteps echoed as someone ascended into my domain. Maeve looked me over when she reached the top of the stairs then set the tray she carried on the table.

I didn't immediately spit out the false thanks she expected, and her expression hardened.

"Where are my manners," I said with a smile. "They seem to have escaped me with all these wondrous thoughts floating in my head. Thank you for feeding me, Mama."

Too much sarcasm laced my words, and her resulting smile should have struck fear in me. I was too blindly angry, though.

"I see."

"I'm glad someone still does."

I turned toward the window.

"You test me?"

Glancing at her, I snorted.

"What will you do? Gouge out my eyes? Drain me of my essence? Walk me naked through the streets? Have men use me and touch me? Cut the hair from my head?" My voice rose with each question. "Do it all! I care not. You've already killed me; my body is only too stupid to die."

The anger immediately left her gaze.

"Then this tray was an unnecessary gesture. Enjoy your solitude."

She took the tray with her as she departed.

I cursed my temper. Though I wasn't the least bit hungry now, I would be tomorrow. And I doubted I would see another tray for some time.

Something crashed from below, and I smiled, hoping it was Maeve. It wasn't right that I should be the only one seething. My smile faded as I realized people tended to die when she was angry. I hurried toward the door, unsure what I could do or say to fix the mess I'd made.

The soft murmur of voices from the vents stopped me.

"...said to her."

I moved closer to Cecilia's vent.

"I don't know. But I've never seen her so angry."

"I didn't know she had the strength to overturn the table."

"You should never doubt Mama's capabilities in anything. Perhaps Eloise did something when Mama told her about the dinner."

I frowned and looked toward the attic door. Maeve had never brought me a tray before. It was always Cecilia or Porcia. How could I have so foolishly not recognized there might have been another reason for her visit?

"Do you think the Prince will turn us away if she's not with us?"

"Don't be silly. If he wanted to dine with Eloise alone, that's what he would have requested."

"I don't know...Kaven's expression was odd when Mama told him Eloise wasn't feeling well and might not be able to attend. I wouldn't be shocked if we receive another message cancelling the invitation before the night is over."

"Nonsense. I can feel tomorrow night will be my opportunity, Porcia. I will beguile the Prince with my womanly charm without Eloise there to distract him."

I quietly moved away from the vent and looked out the window at the fading light. Nothing moved out there. How long ago had Kaven called? I hoped that he didn't believe he'd somehow hurt me with last night's activities. Or worse, that I was avoiding him.

Tired from standing and thinking, I lay on my bed. I didn't bother to light a candle. Staring at the darkness above me, I listened to the bird song fade to be replaced with the occasional hoot of an owl. Below, the house quieted.

Though my day had been long and taxing, I couldn't sleep. In the silence, my mind kept returning to Alfie and dwelled on what I should have tried in order to prevent his fate. Deep down, I knew there was nothing. It had been a test of loyalty, and he had been the only one who knew me. Everyone else was already dead. Except Kellen. Maybe.

Rather than wait for the next tragedy to strike, I rose and padded across the floor in my bare feet. There was only one course of action that was open to me at this point. I needed to go to the tree. I hesitated and looked at the small patch of the outside world visible through the window. Although the hour was late, and this household was abed, would Kaven, too, be sleeping? Or was he wandering the woods in the hopes that I would meet him as I had the night before?

My hand lifted to touch my shorn hair. What excuse could I give for how I looked if he did happen upon me? Perhaps I should wait until tomorrow evening when—I shook my head. Waiting meant that Cecilia would have the Prince alone. He would be unprotected, and so would the kingdom.

Resolved, I snuck through the house and let myself outside. The cool ground anchored me to the moment. For now, I was free to do as I pleased. Free to feel the night wind on my face. Free to ask for help.

The bird in the clearing chirped a quiet greeting.

"Please stay silent for me," I said softly. "I cannot be discovered tonight."

The bird chirped again but did not sing.

I went to stand before the tree and looked up into the blossom laden branches.

"My life is changing faster than I think I can bear. Yet, I know I will. The suffering I've witnessed in Towdown cannot be allowed to continue. Help me to stop it. Please. Help me understand what I must do."

The little bird chirped twice, and the branches shook, raining down petals upon my head. Before me, a light flashed amidst the blossoms. As I watched, a bud rapidly grew on the branch nearest me until one by one the petals of the bloom opened to reveal a silver ring.

I took the ring and turned it in the moonlight. An inlaid

golden crown stood out against the grey. My heart clenched, and I looked at the bird.

"I'm meant to marry him, aren't I?"

In response, the small creature took flight and landed on my finger. It sang a soft song filled with sorrow.

A lone tear trailed down my cheek.

"So be it," I whispered.

CHAPTER THIRTEEN

When the room began to lighten, I sat up with a weary sigh and removed the chamber pot from under my bed. I hadn't lied the day before when I told Maeve she'd killed me. There was nothing left in me for her to hurt or take. My last hidden dream of a life with Kaven was gone, killed by the tree's gift of a groom's ring fit only for a prince.

The numbness and anger that consumed me at all that Maeve had taken or forced upon me left only a mere echo of the girl I used to be.

When I finished with the chamber pot, I went to the washbasin and froze at the sight of my hair in the mirror. Last night when I'd returned from my time with the tree, I'd hidden the ring behind the chimney and washed before changing into my nightgown. My hair had been the same jagged cropping as it had before. Since then, it had grown several inches, almost covering my ears.

I looked horrible, but I grinned. Maeve would be irate when she saw this. She would wonder who had helped me, again, and likely have a fit. I looked around the attic. There was nothing else to find here save the ring, and I'd hidden that higher than I could reach without the assistance of a chair.

Even the thought of waking again in town, naked and sick, couldn't rob me of my humor as I dressed for the day and went to sit at the table. I didn't expect them to feed me this morning and wondered how much longer my hair would grow by the time they did.

Happiness, the true kind that cannot be contained, often made people do strange things. I was no exception. I threw open my window.

"Tis a fine morning, is it not?" I called softly to the birds. I grinned and started singing. It wasn't loud, just a happy song from my childhood. Something Kellen and I would sing while playing in the puddles after a rain. The birds joined me, creating a melody that shook the trees.

From the vents, I heard Cecilia yell for the birds to quiet. Suitably entertained for the morning, I took the book of fairytales and sat in a comfortable chair.

Porcia arrived with a tray near midday. I looked up from my story as she set it on the table.

"Thank you, sister. I'm quite famished."

Ignoring her wide-eyed stare, I pulled the tray close and scooped up a bite of oats.

"You had best fetch her quickly," I said. "She'll want to know." Putting the bite into my mouth, I groaned.

She pivoted and jogged down the stairs. The door closed but no key turned in the lock. I chuckled and began eating faster. It was probably foolish to fill my stomach, given Maeve's new favorite form of punishments, but I was too hungry to care. I'd barely finished my bowl when the door opened below. Pushing the tray aside, I waited. Maeve came alone, her gaze sweeping the room.

"No one came here," I said. "I went to bed shorn and woke like this. Well, not like this. I think it's grown more since waking." I touched the ends that were closer to my jawline than the bottom of my ear now.

She gazed at me thoughtfully.

"Yet, this is not the work of the protection spell as the hair was cut free from your head."

Her gaze swept the room again.

"How do you explain this then?"

"I cannot." For I couldn't. I didn't know how my hair was growing. However, I did have my suspicions. The tree. But I wasn't sure how.

"Very well. What has been undone can be done again."

She left the attic and returned a short while later with Seth and the shears Judith had kept in the kitchen. He approached with a mean look in his eyes.

"I won't struggle against this," I said looking at her. "He doesn't need to hold me."

"I believe he does."

He grabbed my arm and jerked me upright only to throw me toward a chair. I tumbled into it, falling to the floor. His weight landed on top of me.

"Where do you want me to hold her?" he asked.

"Anywhere you would like." She gripped my hair.

His weight shifted, and I felt his hand slide up my leg. The first snick of the shears echoed as I fought to free myself from Seth's hold.

"Foul retch, get off me!"

The speed with which Maeve wielded the shears was the only thing that stopped Seth from reaching my underthings.

"Release her," she said after the final snip.

He immediately obeyed, and I scrambled to my feet. Seth stood far too close, grinning smugly. I stomped on his foot then lifted a knee the moment he widened his stance. He fell to the floor with a grunt and looked up at Maeve as an unnatural flush slowly crept up his face.

I turned to her too, bracing myself for some form of retribution. Instead of directing any anger at me, Maeve arched a brow at Seth.

"I will not reprimand Eloise for that, and neither will you. Next time, take less joy in your task, and stand at a safer distance when finished. And never forget who holds your loyalty. You are mine to use as I see fit."

He nodded and slowly got to his feet. Seth wasn't as fully under her thrall as Hugh had been, for the look he gave me as he left was filled with promised retribution.

The door had hardly been closed for more than a few minutes after their departure when I heard Cecilia's screech of outrage from the vents.

"Cast a truth spell on her."

The sound of Maeve's voice was easily recognizable even if her words were not. I hurried toward the vent, light on my feet.

"I apologize, Mother. I certainly didn't mean for my suggestion to sound like an order. The idea of cancelling our appearance tonight has me distraught. Without her there, this could be my chance to lure the Prince."

"Without her there, this could be your chance to ruin everything as well. I wasn't blind to Kaven's reaction when I said she wouldn't be attending. Rather than provoke suspicion, it's wisest to send our regrets and state we're all feeling ill. It might also help pass any budding suspicion after your foolish sleight of hand with his wine."

I smiled and went back to my book.

MAEVE WAS RUNNING out of excuses, patience, and time, which made her dangerously unpredictable. I sat at the breakfast table, my gaze fixed on the stew before me as I listened to her fingers thrum over the wooden surface.

"We cannot postpone again, Mama," Porcia said softly.

"Do you think I don't know this?"

I could feel her gaze on me.

"I cannot decide if it's the Prince's fascination with you or the servant's that keeps him returning," she said.

My heart ached at the memory of Kaven's face as he'd looked upon me only moments ago. There'd been a desperate need in his eyes that hadn't escaped Maeve's notice. I couldn't begin to suppose what he might have been thinking of my avoidance of him since our time in the woods five nights ago.

"I suppose you think I should be grateful your hair has grown back," Maeve said. The edge to her words kept me silent.

Each morning, she cut my hair only for it to grow back to its old length even faster. This morning, it had only taken two hours.

"I know someone is helping you. These little games will do nothing to stop me from reclaiming what is rightfully mine." She pressed her hands flat against the table. "And when I have what I want, you will be truly punished for every moment of defiance you have shown me."

She hit the table hard.

"Look at me when I'm speaking to you."

I immediately met her gaze. From my peripheral, I could see Porcia's pale and terrified face and Cecilia's carefully blank one.

"I will flay the skin from you piece by piece, starting at your feet. Tell me who is helping you," she demanded.

I thought of Rose and opened my mouth. No sound emerged.

Maeve's face turned red, and I thought she would strike out at Cecilia, who was closest. Instead, she took a few calming breaths.

"Very well. We have a ball to prepare for. Cecilia, have the maids prepare the bath water. Porcia, send Seth to me. I will respond to the Prince that we will dine with him tomorrow. Eloise, back to your room. I will let you out tomorrow morning if one of your sisters is successful tonight. If not, I will ensure you succeed where they failed."

"Yes, Mama," all three of us said at the same time.

I fled quickly, escaping to my sanctuary. My shorn hair from this morning lay scattered near the table. Since that first morning, she hadn't used Seth to hold me down. And I hadn't fought her. There was no point when we both knew it would only grow back.

Going to my bed, I idled away the hours and listened to Cecilia and Porcia prepare for the ball.

There were no giggles and excited chatter this time. Only quiet whispers, which I couldn't even understand when standing directly above the vent.

I was impatient for them to leave so I could go to the tree to change. I needed to arrive at the ball first. My urgency, however, was torn between finding Kaven to apologize and approaching the Prince. How did one ask for a prince's hand in marriage? I wiped my suddenly sweaty palms on my gown and began pacing the floor.

When the hour arrived for my sisters to depart, my door opened once more, and Maeve ascended. In her hand, she held the shears. She looked at the hair I'd piled together from all of the shearings.

"You were restless today. I could hear you walking back and forth. To keep you busy, you will cut your hair tonight each time it grows back. I will check on the size of the pile when I return."

Her words didn't fool me. I knew the task had nothing to do with my restlessness and everything to do with her suspicion I was somehow gaining outside help.

With a racing pulse, I took the shears from her and said a weak, "Yes, Mama."

She nodded and left me, locking the door behind her.

I looked down at the shears and debated cutting away my hair now. If I did, it wouldn't regrow quickly enough to disguise me at the ball. If I didn't... I looked at the small mound of hair by the window. Given the hour and how quickly it had grown this morning, I wouldn't have a big enough pile by the time she returned. She would either believe I had disobeyed or that I had left to find help again. Both would lead to a worse fate if I failed to gain the Prince's affection tonight.

So, I couldn't fail.

Tossing the shears aside, I fetched the key and made my way downstairs. A soft noise from the dining room sent my heart racing. I looked around in panic and hurried to the wall near the dining room door.

"You want to go in the mistress's room or the older miss's?" one of the maids asked.

"Neither. Both make me feel as if I'm being watched."

"It's probably the one in the attic, peering through the floorboards."

They both left the dining room, focused on their conversation, and made their way to the stairs. I held my breath until they reached the landing and turned their backs to me. Heart racing, I slipped into the dining room and hurried for the kitchen door. Only when I reached the trees, could I draw a decent breath again.

Picking up my skirts, I ran along the path until I arrived in the clearing. The tree started to shiver as soon as I approached. I stood under its limbs as petals rained down on me and a light grew brightly in its branches.

When the dress fell, over half the branches were barren. After the shoes and mask fell, very little remained. With the dress bundled in my arms, I leaned my forehead against the trunk as it began to split.

"For all that you've already done and given me, I am forever grateful. Let us both hope tonight will be the end of this, and I will do what must be done."

The bird began to tap the wood impatiently, this time stopping at eleven.

I stepped back and began to strip from my gown.

"I will leave before the bells toll for the eleventh hour."

Standing in my shift, I shook out the dress and stared in awe at what the tree had created for me. The material seemed spun of silver and stitched with threads of gold. The colors glinted and played off one another in the moonlight. Hurrying, I dressed and marveled at the full skirt and elegant design that left much of my back exposed. The shoes, like the dress, were of both silver and gold. But, it was the mask that really drew my attention. Golden feathers swept out from the side, drawing one's attention to the diminutive golden beak that covered the top portion of my nose.

Silence filled the clearing, and I looked up to see the glimmer of the garden between its two halves. I quickly tied the mask in place and stepped through the shimmer. The soft strands of music greeted me on the other side.

Sparing no time to marvel at the beauty around me, I hastened from the water and across the lawn. People mingled just on the other side of the hedges and upon the steps. A few paused in the middle of whatever they were saying to stare at my sudden appearance. I didn't stop or offer any more than a hasty smile.

Couples were already dancing, but the ballroom didn't seem as crowded as it had been the time before. I'd almost made it across the space when an arm caught me around the waist.

"End my torment and dance with me," Kaven said in my ear.

I froze, heart beating hard as my chest tightened. I wanted nothing more than to idle away the hours in his arms. Closing my eyes against the pain, I shook my head.

"I cannot. I must see the Prince."

He turned me, and I forced myself to meet his gaze.

"Why?" he asked softly, taking my hand in his. Just the simple touch of his fingers against mine was enough to dampen some of my hurry.

"I'm supposed to present myself to the court first, not after I dance the night away."

"Hmm." He pulled me closer. "Are you sure? I don't recall a proclamation stating such."

I swallowed hard when he turned us into the dancers, joining their sweeping moves.

"Please, Kaven," I said softly. "Do not make this more difficult than it already is." The pain in my middle grew. "I cannot spend all my time with you."

"And why not? Am I not good enough for you?"

"For me, you are the sun and moon and stars. You bring light into my life where there is otherwise none."

His steps slowed.

"You need more time," he said.

"I need understanding," I said, for no amount of time would change what needed to be.

He sighed.

"I will take you, then."

We stopped spinning, and he offered his arm. I set my hand on it, hoping he wouldn't note the tremble. People watched us as we crossed the room.

I glanced at Kaven. Dressed in a white jacket trimmed with gold, he was a dashing figure.

"Is that a real gold mask?" I asked, noting the etchings on the otherwise unadorned surface.

"It is."

"Does it bother you to wear such riches frivolously when so many go hungry less than a catapult's throw from the castle?"

He glanced at me.

"Does it bother you to wear your frivolities?"

I looked down at the dress.

"Bother doesn't sufficiently describe how very much what I'm wearing disturbs me."

When I looked up at him, he was frowning.

"Why did you wear it then?"

"Because I must."

"As must I."

His words only served as a reminder of what I was about to do. He was a servant of the Prince. The very man I was about to openly proposition. It would break Kaven. But no more than it would break me.

Instead of going to the ornate doors of the court, he veered to one of the side halls. The guards who stood there nodded and let us pass.

"You're shaking," Kaven said, placing his hand over mine.

"We've just crossed into a part of the castle where guests are discouraged from going. By sword point. Of course I'm shaking."

He chuckled and led me toward a set of stairs protected by two more of the King's guard. They, too, nodded as we passed and began to ascend.

"There is nothing to worry about," he assured me. "You'll be welcomed."

He stopped in front of a plain door and knocked softly.

"Enter," a deep voice called.

Kaven opened the door and bade me to enter. Inside, the King stood by the fire, striking a pose so similar to the one I'd seen his son strike countless times before.

"Your Majesties, may I present to you Eloise Cartwright, Margaret Cartwright's daughter."

I gave a deep curtsy. The Prince, who had been sitting in a chair near his father, rose with a smile.

"Eloise," he said. "This is a welcome and pleasant surprise. You just saved me from a long lecture regarding my duties tonight."

The King harrumphed.

"Hardly a lecture. However, your presence is welcome, Miss Cartwright."

The King nodded at me and looked at Kaven.

"If Miss Cartwright can spare your presence," the King said, "we need to speak about tonight's plans."

"Of course, Sire," I said quickly.

Kaven waited for the King to precede him out the door, then left me alone with the Prince. The opportunity couldn't have been more perfect. When I turned, I gave a startled laugh at how closely the Prince now stood.

"I apologize," he said quickly. "I only wanted to thank you again for your timely intervention. You seem to have a knack for it."

"I am at your service. Always." I took a calming breath. "Which is why I insisted on speaking with you."

"Oh? How can I help you?"

He took my hand and set it on his arm to lead me to a seat.

"It's I who can help you," I said, as I turned toward him as he sat beside me. "For the sake of the kingdom, I will wed you if you would have me."

His brows rose, and he coughed out a laugh.

"I don't think Kaven would approve of your offer. Or my father."

"I don't see why not. Your father wants you to wed and produce an heir for the safety of the kingdom. Unless some maid has already ensnared your interest, I see no reason for your father to disapprove of our union. By your own words, my family is in good standing with the Crown, and I know I can pass all the tests required."

His humor faded in the face of my earnestness.

"Why would you do this?"

"For the sake of the kingdom and all those who fall under its rule. I've seen too much suffering to do nothing."

He glanced away, looking at the fire.

"Your offer is unexpected but not unwelcome. I will need some time to consider it."

"Of course. I will see myself to the main ballroom."

He nodded absently, and I left the room. A door down, the murmur of Kaven's voice drew my attention. I hesitated, wondering if I should wait for him to finish his discussion with the King or leave on my own. After my talk with the Prince, I wanted to leave without facing Kaven. But it would be cruel to let him hear of my proposal from the Prince instead of an explanation from my own lips.

I approached the door and heard more than I should.

"...send her away. You know what's at stake."

"Father, please. The longer we wait—"

"Greydon, enough," the King said sharply.

Unable to help myself, I moved forward until I could see around the partially closed door. I stared at the room's only two occupants in horror as pain sliced through my heart and robbed me of air. There was no mistake in whom the King addressed as Greydon or who Kaven had just addressed as Father.

CHAPTER FOURTEEN

THE KING SIGHED WEARILY AND GRIPPED HIS SON'S shoulder, both still unaware of my presence in the hall.

"I understand your concerns. The girl is lovely, no doubt, but she needs to leave. Immediately. The castle is the last place she should be seen."

Deceived. Used. Now, cast aside. Crushing the soft material in my fisted hands, I lifted my skirts and stepped away from the door.

The hallway suddenly felt too narrow, and I struggled to breathe as I hurried back the way I'd come.

"Eloise," the Prince said, emerging from his room just as I'd passed it.

Turning slowly, I looked at the imposter.

"What's happened?" he asked, moving toward me. "You're pale. Are you hurt?"

I flinched back when he reached for me.

"Do not touch me. Is it you I should call Kaven? Or is that name nothing more than a figment to fool simple maids?"

His hand dropped to his side.

"I see."

"I do not. What a jest my offer must have been for you. What new cruelty will I face on the morrow?"

"Eloise, it's not what you think."

"I believe it is." In my eyes, the King and his son were no different than Maeve and her daughters.

"I'm Garreth, second in line for the Crown, after my brother, Greydon. I stand in his place to protect him from those who are trying to cause him harm."

Behind him, Kaven—no, Greydon—stepped into the hall. He frowned when he saw me.

"She knows," the Prince said.

"Yes," I said softly. "She knows."

Fear lit in Kaven's eyes—I closed mine briefly, forcing myself to acknowledge there was no Kaven. Only Greydon.

When I opened them, Greydon was striding toward me. I shook my head, turned, and ran.

"Eloise, wait!"

His footfalls echoed behind me. So much anger gave me the will necessary to keep ahead of him. I sped the length of the hall and down the stairs, almost losing a shoe. The guards stepped toward me.

"Do not touch her," Greydon commanded. "Eloise, let me explain."

Every vile name I could think of bubbled up in my mind as I recalled the night we'd spent together. I'd thrown myself at him. What a fool I'd been. Prince Greydon had never been in danger. They'd been using Garreth to draw Maeve and her daughters out. Much like me, Garreth was the sacrifice.

"Stop this foolishness," he said as I reached the end.

Oh, I am, I thought silently.

The next set of guards didn't even hear me until I burst into the main hall filled with masked people, all gaily enjoying the commencement of the third ball. Those nearest the private hall hurriedly parted to make way for me. That commotion caused those between me and the exit to step aside.

I could hear Greydon behind me, but he didn't call my name or demand I be stopped. He didn't need to. He knew where I lived.

Reaching the outer doors, I panted for air and lifted my skirts higher to sprint down the steps. Below, I saw the familiar faces of Cecilia and Porcia. Faltering, I almost lost my balance. Instead, I lost a shoe.

Desperation saw me to the bottom, and I slipped from the castle grounds into the night.

NUMB, I listened to the snick of the shears and pulled another clump of hair forward. The golden strands fell victim to the sharp metal edges and floated to the floor with the rest.

I only did as Maeve had told me because I didn't know what else to do. I'd returned to the tree and cried at its roots. After removing my ballgown and tossing it into the branches, I'd redressed and returned to my room undetected. Emotionally raw at the betrayal of the Royal family and everyone else in my life, I struggled to form a single reasonable thought.

Why had Kaven kept everything from me? Why tell me I would be his forever when he had no right to make such promises? It didn't matter that I'd been of a mind not to accept his promise. I had pushed aside my own desire for happiness to help the people, offering him only one night together, nothing more. And, it didn't matter that I'd kept truths from him as well. It was only the spell and the need to protect him that kept me silent.

Out of hair, I lowered my hands and let my arms rest for a few minutes. My scalp tingled as the new hair rapidly grew. How many times had I cut every strand from my head? I looked down at the hair circling my chair. Many times from the looks of it.

The rattle of the carriage announced the return of those who had created all of my woes. Lifting my arms, I snicked away at my hair again. Silence continued in the house, but I wasn't lulled by it. And the sound of my door opening several moments later wasn't unexpected.

"Eloise, come down here."

"Yes, Mama," I said, immediately standing and setting the shears aside. My scalp tingled on the right half of my head, already regrowing what I'd clipped away.

Maeve stood at the bottom of the stairs, her eyes cold as she watched me descend. Her gaze flicked briefly to my hair. She said nothing about it as she turned and bade for me to follow.

Below, Porcia and Cecilia waited in the sitting room. Both seemed more subdued than usual.

"What happened?" I asked, trying to sound as if I cared. It was difficult to do when everything inside of me felt dead and heavy.

"The mystery maiden was there," Maeve said. "She ran from the ball, chased by the Prince's servant. Show me your feet."

I blinked in confusion and lifted my nightgown to peek at my own feet. They were clean despite running without a shoe.

"All of you," Maeve said impatiently. I looked at Porcia and Cecilia in confusion as they hurried to remove their stocking and shoes. "Line up with your sister. It's no wonder the Prince wasn't interested in the pair of you. You don't even have a full thought put together."

When the three of us stood in a row, Maeve studied our feet.

"Cecilia, yours might be a bit too long. You will need to cut away some of your heel. Porcia, yours are too wide. Likely all those years of overindulging your sweets. Cut away your little toe."

Porcia paled, and Maeve stepped before me.

"It always seems to come back to you, doesn't it, Eloise?" she said.

"I don't understand. Why do our feet matter?"

"Because the Prince has decreed he will have no other for his bride but the runaway maiden."

My stomach twisted. What was Greydon thinking?

"Since she is a mystery, a Royal procession will go from home to home with the slipper she lost tonight on the stairs. The maid who fits the slipper and can produce its match will be queen."

I now understood why she wanted Porcia and Cecilia to cut away bits of themselves. But why look at my feet?

"You think the shoe will fit me?" I asked, dread settling into my stomach.

"I was able to pick it up and study it for a moment before the Prince's servant took it in the name of the Crown. Yes, I believe it will fit you. But only if it does not fit my more obedient daughters first."

"How will you produce its match?"

"Don't worry about that. I always find a way. Go to your room and clean up the hair. Don't cut it again until the queen is chosen."

I nodded and hurried away.

In my room, I gathered up the hair in a spare bedsheet. Descending again, I found Maeve in the entry, staring at the place the mirror once resided. She turned at the sound of my approach.

She glanced at the bundle and pointed to the kitchen.

"Throw it in the fire. Hair burns quickly."

The sound of soft sobs coming from the direction of the kitchen made my stomach twist sickeningly as if I'd crossed the estate's boundaries. However, given Maeve's current mood, I didn't dare disobey.

With a quiet, "Yes, Mama," I left her in the entry and went to join my sisters in the kitchen.

"Stop crying," Cecilia said harshly as I opened the door.

Porcia looked up at me, her eyes red and her cheeks tear stained. At her feet, Cecilia knelt with a paring knife in her hand.

"What do you want?" she demanded.

"Mama told me to burn my hair." I quickly turned my back to them.

"It should be you who needs the knife," she said angrily. "Not us. We've always obeyed."

My skin crawled with disgust. It was their willingness to do whatever Maeve wanted and their perverse need for power that put them where they were. I held no pity for them.

"I'll slice along the side of the toe and cut it from the joint. It will leave more skin to sew it closed."

Not wanting to stay and witness what they were about to do, I threw the whole balled up sheet into the fire. It caught within moments, and the eye-watering stench of burning hair drove me from the room before Cecilia made the first cut.

I PACED THE FLOOR, watching the sky lighten. No one had come to lock my door last night, and I wasn't sure if that meant I was to go downstairs for breakfast or remain where I was. I would much prefer the latter. Solitude felt like a balm as I speculated the different outcomes for Greydon's newest deception.

It wasn't until I'd returned to my room the evening before that I gave the reason behind the proclamation any thought. He knew to whom the slipper belonged, so the proclamation was a trap for those who meant the Crown harm. Of course, many maids would fit the shoe. It was the maid who was not me, but able to produce the match, who would reveal herself as the caster. Would it be enough, though? Without a doubt, Maeve would see to it that Cecilia or Porcia would fit the shoe. But would her magic be able to recreate the missing shoe? And if so, would Greydon know it wasn't just the maid but the mother and sister as well? If not, I doubted I would be able to condemn them all with the spell still holding me mute. And, if

Maeve wasn't condemned, she would still be free to find another way to get what she wanted.

I glanced at the chimney where the ring still remained hidden. The tree meant for me to wed Prince Greydon. Of that I was certain. I'd been willing to give myself over to the Prince because, arrogance aside, I'd thought him honest. But last night's revelation had me questioning everything, including how far I was willing to go to save a people who didn't even know me. I'd walked through Towdown naked, and only one person had stepped forward to help me.

Why should I give so much for so very little in return? And I most certainly did not aspire to someday become a queen. While the position might offer some privilege, it offered far more obligation.

I thought back to when Kellen and I roamed as we would, free of responsibility and pain, and the desire to return to the days before Mother died overwhelmed me.

"There has to be another way," I whispered.

I didn't believe in fate. It was an excuse for those who didn't have the will to fight for what they wanted. I had will and then some. And I wanted the freedom to choose my own future.

Outside, early morning sunlight glinted through the treetops. I had time. No one, save the maids, ever rose so early. Decided, I hurried to escape my attic refuge. The house was quiet on the second floor, and I softly closed my door to tiptoe down the stairs. If I hurried, I could return from the clearing and be the first in the dining room.

The birds greeted me with a cheery song as I ran along the path. The cool morning air filled me with life and energy. I wished more than anything I could continue running through the trees. Run all the way to the Dark Forest and scream Kellen's name until she heard me.

Instead, I burst into Mother's clearing and fell to my knees at the base of the tree.

"There must be another way," I begged. "I cannot do what you want. Please."

The bird chirped from a branch, its song distressed.

"You don't understand. Everything has been a lie. Lies on top of lies. That isn't the life I want. I will not accept it."

The tree shivered and shook and above me a single bud appeared. It grew in size until its petals opened one by one. From inside, another ring fell into my hand.

With a sinking heart, I looked at the elegant ring. Smaller than the first, the band of silver was much thinner and more ornately carved. Instead of a gold crown, this one had a crown of diamond with sapphire chips at each peak. It was the female match to the male ring I already had. This one was meant for me.

I fisted my hand around the ring and drew back my arm to throw the unwanted jewelry into the woods. I would not do as it wanted.

A hand closed over mine.

Shocked, I looked up at Maeve as she pried my fingers apart. She took the ring and looked up at the tree.

"How is this possible? Who enchanted this tree?"

I scrambled to my feet, fear and anger loosening my tongue and spurring me to speak without first considering my words.

"Father gave me a pear tree shoot the day before we buried my mother. Once touched by—" My throat closed over the word.

"The magic from the amulet?" Maeve said, guessing what I meant to say.

I nodded.

"When I planted it here, I think what had touched her lingered and touched the tree."

"How does it work?"

In that moment, I knew I couldn't tell her. What would Maeve ask for? What would the tree give?

I stared at her defiantly, and she grabbed my arm.

"Do not think the Prince's affection for the manservant will stay my hand a second time. Tell me."

My mind raced. The manservant wasn't unprotected like she thought. Had I paid more attention during our night together, I felt certain I would have noted an amulet. However, even if she couldn't hurt him, she could still take her anger out on others. And, the tree never gave me what I wanted but what it thought I needed to stop her.

"I ask the tree for what I need, and it falls from the branches," I said, hoping I was right that the tree wouldn't help her.

Maeve released me and looked up at the budding leaves.

"I need a way to see those who seek to stop me from gaining the throne."

The little bird chirped in its nest and took flight. I watched it disappear into the forest, heading toward Towdown.

"Well?" Maeve said impatiently, still staring up in the branches.

"I don't think it's going to work. The bird flew away."

"You said it was the tree who granted you what you wanted."

I shook my head.

"It grants me what I need, not what I want. And the bird is always there. It's never flown away before."

Her cold gaze went to the ring in her hand before locking onto me.

"And what else has the tree given you?"

"A mask and a dress and shoes to match."

Her eyes widened in understanding, and she struck out, slapping me hard. My head jerked with the impact.

"You thought to use my power against me?" she demanded.

"Yes," I said simply, holding her gaze.

Her eyes narrowed on me.

"Where is the other shoe?"

"I gave it back to the tree when I returned."

She looked at the tree and put her hand to her chest.

"Let tinder burn to nothing but cinder. That made of gold, silver, or glass let the fire bypass."

With a flash of green light, the tree ignited. I grabbed Maeve's arm angrily.

"Without the tree, you have no hope of producing the matching shoe."

She struck me again, the impact sending me to the ground.

"Do not presume to admonish me," she yelled. "If the tree still holds the shoe, the flames will not touch it. If the tree does not, I have no use for it. And neither do you."

With tears filling my eyes, I watched my mother's tree, my father's last gift to me, burn to nothing in mere minutes. Maeve grabbed me and pushed me into the coal.

"Dig in the ashes. Find the shoe."

I shifted through the hot coals, my slippers burning away along with the base of my dress. The heat didn't touch my skin, though. I dug and dug but found no shoe. I did, however, find the remnants of the bird's little nest, filled with red hot coals. I swallowed hard, trying to tamp down the anger that shook my limbs.

Why was I listening to Maeve? To protect two maids I didn't even know? I was done trying to think rationally and keep my temper under control.

With an angry cry, I stood and threw a fistful of hot coals at Maeve. They scattered, hitting her face and bodice. Instead of crying out in pain, she laughed and brushed away the coals.

"I thought the spell of protection quite clever and decided I needed one for myself."

She stalked toward me and grabbed my arm.

"Is there anything else you would care to try?"

"Yes."

I punched her right in the mouth.

She laughed, and I tumbled headlong into oblivion.

CHAPTER FIFTEEN

WAKING FROM MAEVE'S SPELL WASN'T LIKE WAKING FROM
sleep. There was no hazy unclarity or pleasant restfulness.
Rather, it was an instant awareness.

A clatter of noise rose outside.

Opening my eyes, the familiar sight of my attic space
greeted me. However, the day's fading light cast shadows in
the room.

I sat up and scanned myself, finding I still wore the
charred remnants of my dress. That didn't make sense. I'd
thrown coal at Maeve's face, and when that hadn't worked,
I'd hit her. I wasn't foolish enough to believe either act
would go unpunished. Yet, I was still clothed and
comfortable on my bed instead of in a hovel in Towdown.

What did Maeve have planned now?

Hurrying from the bed, I moved to stand, and my eyes
caught on the two dresses laying on the table I used for my

solitary meals. Maid's dresses. And shoes. But the shoes were standing upright as if still—

A small pained sound escaped me as I recognized the shriveled twisted remains of the two maids. Throat tight and tears wetting my lashes, I went to them. How could I have been so foolish? I'd known what would happen and had acted rashly, regardless of the consequences.

A note waited on the chest of one. I picked it up and read the brief scrawl.

THEIR LIVES *for your defiance and a shoe. Clean yourself and join us in the sitting room, or more will follow.*

TEARS SPILLED over as the sounds in the yard continued.

"Poor Catherine and Heather," I said softly. "Killed twice over and for what? Her petty need for retribution."

I set my hand on the skirt of one. I wasn't even sure which it was.

"Rest peacefully, knowing that I am not yet finished. I will give my dying breath to see her fall. She will suffer for all that she's done."

Wiping my eyes, I noted the washbowl and gown that waited on the chair near the table. The dress wasn't one I recognized as belonging to Cecilia or Porcia. Holding it up to me, I found the length perfect, which meant Maeve had it made for me at some point. The knowledge that she still thought to use me grated at my raw nerves. I looked down at my ragged skirt and, for the briefest of moments, considered leaving it on. However, her note clearly stated what the outcome of such defiance would be.

"Eloise Cartwright," a male voice called from below. "We await your presence."

Stripping from the remnants of my gown, I quickly washed my face then changed. While I laced the dress, I struggled to piece together what Maeve might intend. She'd kept me under her spell for the majority of the day, only to wake me now when we had guests. Not a few but many from the sounds of the horses outside. And, the authority that clearly rang in the voice that just called to me could only mean one thing. The Prince and his contingent were here because of the proclamation.

My mind raced with my feet. When I reached the top of the main staircase, I stopped and stared at all of the men I glimpsed through the open entry door. A veritable army.

"Miss Cartwright?" a voice asked.

"Yes," I said, looking at the older man who waited at the bottom of the stairs. He wasn't dressed as a guard but wore a fine jacket to rival any I saw on the King.

"Your mother and sisters are waiting for you."

I slowly descended and took his arm, letting him escort me into the sitting room. Two guards stood sentinel just inside the door.

Standing before the fire, Prince Garreth's presence was

as stately as ever. When he glanced at me, his gaze gave nothing away.

Maeve, sitting in a chair nearest to the door, smiled when I entered.

"There you are darling. You've kept the Prince waiting."

I ignored her admonishment and looked at Cecilia and Porcia, who sat on a settee near the Prince. Porcia looked pale, her upper lip glistening. Cecilia looked unaffected by whatever she'd done to herself.

The final occupant in the room stood by the chair across from the pair. The chair to which I was being led. My heart started to race, and I refused to look at Greydon, who watched my approach. Instead, I focused on the firelight that glinted off the original slipper he held displayed prominently on a silken cushion.

In everything that had happened, I hadn't considered the impossibility of carrying out the proclamation. The slipper should have vanished at the eleventh hour like its partner. How was it still here? I thought of the ring in the attic and the one Maeve took, no longer sure what rules applied to the items given by the tree.

"Are there any other maidens in the house?" the older man asked after I sat.

"No, Lord Firth," Maeve said. "None."

"Very well. This day has been long as you can imagine. Now that all the maidens are present, we must ask if you have the match to this shoe."

There was a rustle of sound near my head, and Cecilia gasped.

"You recognize it, miss?" the older man asked.

"I do. Alas, I no longer have the match. It was broken in my race from the castle."

Doubt clouded the man's eyes.

"As we've heard many times today."

"And did the shoe fit those maids?"

"They did not," he said, reluctantly.

"Then allow me to prove to you that the shoe is mine."

Greydon stepped forward with the slipper, and my heart lurched at the sight of his broad shoulders as he passed the cushion to Lord Firth. The man knelt before Cecilia and removed her slipper. I watched in horror as my shoe easily slid into place over her foot.

She smiled brilliantly at Garreth.

"It fits," she said.

"So it does," he said calmly.

A bird flew into the room, startling us all.

"Check her heel while you kneel," it sang before flying from the room just as quickly as it had come.

Lord Firth glanced at Garreth, who nodded. Cecilia quickly removed her foot from his hold.

"Surely you're not going to believe an enchanted bird?" she said. "The creature itself is treachery."

"Remove the shoe and allow Lord Firth to inspect your foot without stocking."

"Sire," Maeve said, looking every inch the outraged mother. "Such a thing is highly improper."

"No more than choosing a bride solely based on her ability to wear a shoe. Don't you agree?" the Prince asked smoothly.

Maeve inclined her head, and I felt a burst of triumph as Lord Firth removed her shoe and stocking to find a good portion of her heel missing.

"I fell from our horse before the ball and hurt myself," Cecilia said quietly.

"Then you cannot be the one for surely you could not run in the shoe."

"But I can." She grabbed the shoe from Lord Firth and stuck her foot into it. "Watch."

She stood and, lifting her skirts, took her first running step. She made it three more before she began limping, and several more after that before the shoe became so slick with blood that it fell from her foot.

"Sit," Garreth commanded.

Ashen, Cecilia sat beside Porcia. I risked a glance at Maeve as Lord Firth removed the shoe and wiped it clean. Nothing showed in her expression, but I didn't miss the slight restlessness of her finger tapping at the arm of her chair.

"What of you, Porcia?" the Prince asked, drawing my attention to her. "Do you believe this to be your shoe?"

If possible, she paled further.

"Yes, Sire," she said quietly.

Lord Firth sighed and knelt by her feet. Her wince when he slid the shoe on was visible to all.

"It fits," Lord Firth said when she remained silent.

"What have you to say about that?" Garreth asked her.

Before she could answer, the bird swooped into the room again.

"Check her toe before you go."

Maeve's eyes tracked its progress as it flew out the door once more. Anger boiled just beneath the surface. She was failing, and she knew it. Her gaze shifted, and her eyes met mine. She visibly relaxed, and a small smile curled her lips.

Turning away from her, I watched as Lord Firth removed the shoe and Porcia's stocking. She offered no explanation for her missing small toe.

"It's been missing since birth and often gives her trouble," Maeve said. "I know the proclamation said no maid with disadvantage, but surely it only meant of face and figure, not foot."

"Will you persist and watch your daughter further injure herself when I insist she must prove she can run in the shoe?" Garreth asked, a note of annoyance creeping into his voice.

"No, your majesty," Maeve said meekly. "But I ask that you allow Eloise an opportunity to try the shoe before you leave."

I met Garreth's questioning gaze as Lord Firth gently removed the shoe from Porcia's now bleeding foot.

"Do you claim this shoe to be yours, Eloise?" His voice

lacked any of the impatience it held when speaking to my step sisters.

"I cannot claim it as mine, for it is not."

Silence fell. I could feel Greydon's gaze on me but refused to look at him.

"What are you saying?" Garreth asked. "You do not wish to try the shoe?"

"Eloise didn't mean that, Your Majesty," Maeve said quickly, rising to stand beside my chair. With her hand resting lightly on my shoulder, she clarified, "She only meant she borrowed the shoe from her sisters. Isn't that right, Eloise?"

I looked at my hands and wondered what would happen to the people in the room if I said no. She couldn't kill Greydon and Garreth, but what of Lord Firth and the guards? She would care nothing for any of them.

Lifting my foot, I remained silent.

"There," Maeve said. "She's willing."

"Allow me," Greydon said, taking the shoe from Lord Firth.

Maeve's fingers twitched on my shoulder as Greydon knelt at my feet and lifted my skirt. He looked up at me, and I averted my gaze to look at Cecilia and Porcia. Porcia trembled in her seat. Cecilia appeared no more composed than her sister.

The shoe slipped easily onto my foot.

"It fits," Greydon said softly.

My heart stuttered for a moment. Clenching my fists in

my lap, I set my foot on the ground and met Greydon's gaze.

"I will not wed Prince Greydon," I said.

Maeve laughed.

"She jests, Your Majesty."

I opened my mouth to damn us all with my further objection when the bird flew into the room again. Surprised, I watched it, wondering if it would accuse me of lies like it had Porcia and Cecilia. However, its words weren't about me as it circled the room.

"She comes! She comes!"

When it returned to the doorway, the guards were gone, and a figure with a familiar dirty cloak stood there.

"Have I come at a bad time to collect my pig?" Rose asked, glancing around the room.

"Not at all," I said quickly. I started to stand, ready for the escape she offered, when Maeve's hand closed over my shoulder.

"What pig?" Maeve asked.

"The pig in the yard. The one I left in Eloise's care the day her mother met the earth."

I saw the moment Maeve's eyes narrowed with suspicion, and I quickly shook my head at Rose. The old woman didn't seem to notice, though.

"Take your pig with my blessing and leave," Maeve said.

Rose shook her head as she smiled at Maeve.

"I couldn't do that without thanking Eloise for her tender care of such a wretched beast." Rose's bright blue gaze swept the room before landing on me. "He said you walked him when you could and never overfed him. More importantly, he said you protected him." She chuckled lowly, and Maeve released my arm.

"You are addled, old woman. Pigs do not speak. Remove yourself from my house."

Rose continued as if Maeve hadn't spoken.

"He asked that I apologize on his behalf for leading you to the bodies of your friends. I believe your grief truly moved him. He seems changed now. Oh, not enough for me to release him of his curse. He will need to do much more than show sympathy for others."

"Curse?" Greydon asked, stepping in front of Garreth.

"Call your guards, Your Majesty," Maeve said, also backing away from Rose. "The one who seeks to harm you has exposed herself."

"Indeed, she has," Rose said with a laugh.

"Guards!" Garreth called.

There was no answering rush of footsteps. Not even a rustle of noise.

"Caster," Maeve said harshly. "You will be hanged."

Rose laughed and held out her hand to me.

"Come here, child."

"No, Eloise," Greydon said. "Stay as you are."

Weary of all that I'd suffered and desperate for it to end no matter what the outcome, I stood.

"Eloise, don't!" Maeve said sharply. "You risk everything."

Ignoring her and Greydon, I went to Rose. The old woman's warm fingers closed around mine, and she smiled. A sense of peace settled over me.

"I'm sorry it took so long," she said. "Some evils hide themselves too well, and I had to be sure of the one with which I was dealing. I truly regret anything you may have suffered."

I gave a choked laugh that was closer to a sob, and Rose gave me a pitying look.

"I surmise it was much, then?"

I opened my mouth, but my words stuck in my throat, robbing me of air.

"Still held by her curse, I see."

Rose looked at Maeve.

"Release her," she said.

"I will not lose what is mine," Maeve replied with cold anger.

My gaze flew to her just as a green glow began to consume her bodice with blinding brilliance.

"Enough," Rose said sharply.

The light died, and Maeve's face turned to one of shock.

With a wave of Rose's hand, thin silver chains appeared at Maeve's feet and slowly wrapped their way up her torso. Maeve's eyes narrowed, and twice more, a light sparked from her amulet, only to sputter and die.

"Fetch her trinket, Eloise," Rose said. "I would get it myself, but young men with less than six inches of steel are worrisome. They always overcompensate with their zealousness."

I wasn't quite sure what she meant by that until I turned and saw both Greydon and Garreth brandishing small blades. Their gazes darted between me, Rose, and Maeve, who was precariously balanced on her feet.

Maeve glowered at me as I crossed the room and hooked my finger on her chain to pull the amulet from her cleavage.

Greydon swore.

Removing the ornament from around her neck, I turned to Rose.

"It's not for me to break," she said.

I looked down at the amulet that had caused me so much pain then crossed the room to Cecilia and Porcia. Both surrendered their amulets without protest. When I had all three, I set them on the floor, along with the shoe.

"Nor are they mine to break," I said, finally meeting Greydon's gaze.

"I believe they're yours, Prince Greydon. For all that was done to your family before it was done to mine."

"Eloise..." The apology in his gaze only hurt me further.

Turning from him, I went to Rose.

"No," Maeve said softly from behind me. "It cannot be."

It wasn't until that moment that I realized what I'd revealed.

"It is," Greydon said.

There was a sound of metal upon stone, and Maeve

screamed. I glanced back and saw Greydon had broken her amulet with the fire poker. With defeated expressions, Cecilia and Porcia sat on the couch and watched him destroy theirs as well.

"Come, child," Rose said. "We should check on the guards."

"Caster, you are not going anywhere," Greydon said. "By the King's order—"

"I'm banished. I know."

"Not until the role you've played in this is clear."

Rose's gaze flicked to me, and I knew she wanted me to speak on her behalf. But I couldn't, not with her spell keeping me silent.

"Release me," I said.

She smiled, and a tingle started in my chest, spreading outward. I faced Greydon.

"Her role has been that of my protector when I could not protect myself."

"Protect you from what?"

I opened my mouth but no words emerged. The slight tightening in my throat warned me not to try too hard. Maeve's spell still held, despite the broken amulet Greydon now held.

He frowned at my continued silence.

"Who arrived first?" he asked. "The woman behind you or your stepmother?"

"Rose did."

"How then can you truly believe that your stepmother acted alone? They are both casters."

Rose stepped forward.

"And how do you propose I prove my innocence when I'm unaware of what you find me guilty of?"

I glanced at Rose.

"He thinks you killed his wife and my mother."

"And do you think that?" she asked me.

"No."

"I wonder why that is. Is it perhaps that you know who did kill his wife and your mother?"

"I cannot say."

"You do not know?"

"I did not say that."

"Ah." Her gaze flicked to Maeve. "Is that woman truly your stepmother?"

"She is. I saw the signed document myself."

"Do you care for her?"

I said nothing.

"Has she mistreated you?"

Rose knew well the answer to that, and she smiled at me when I remained mute.

"There is so much more to this story, Your Majesty," she said turning to Greydon, "and Eloise is the key. Not I. However, I've decided to remain until everything is revealed."

"Then, I must insist you accompany us to the castle. My father, King Aftan, will want to speak with you."

She inclined her head.

"I will meet you at the gates."

With that, the old woman disappeared. Moments later, guards rushed into the room.

Maeve, Porcia, and Cecilia were quickly taken outside, and I was jostled aside. I didn't care. The faster everyone left my home, the faster I could put the past several months behind me. The thought fractured me. How could I possibly move on?

Arms closed around my waist, and I found myself up in Greydon's arms before I knew his intent.

"Put me down."

"There is still the matter of the shoe," he said.

"The matter is settled for I have given my answer," I said. "If the kingdom is still in need of a queen, find another gullible maid."

I turned away from his pleading gaze as he stepped outside with me.

"I care not for what the kingdom's need for a queen might be, but my own," he said softly.

He brought me to a horse and helped me into the saddle. When he moved to join me, I planted my bare foot in his chest.

"Find another."

He scowled at me.

"I made you a promise," he said.

"To leave me alone forever?" I said sweetly.

"To be patient. To give you time. But, I also swore you

were mine. Who I am changes nothing about how I feel for you."

"It changes everything for me."

I dug my heels into the steed, desperate to leave Greydon and put an end to the charade I'd been living.

CHAPTER SIXTEEN

AFTER RACING FROM THE ESTATE'S BOUNDARIES AND ALMOST falling off the horse because of the resulting violent heaving, I returned to the yard, ignored Greydon's puzzled frown, and took a position just behind Maeve and her daughters. Maeve smirked knowingly but said nothing about my presence.

The ploddingly slow journey to the castle grated at me on many fronts. Maeve was caught and in chains—the magical links having slithered high enough up her gown to allow her to walk. Her amulet had been stripped from her. I should have been free, but I wasn't. Wouldn't that mean Maeve still had power? I opened my mouth to question the nearest guard but choked on my words. How could I be so close to freedom and still be every inch Maeve's prisoner?

Glaring, I watched Maeve walk proudly, her head high as if she weren't plodding along the dirt path after dark like some common woman. Beside her mother, Cecilia limped heavily. Her determination to keep pace was etched in every line of her cold, regal expression. It was Porcia who slowed the party with her staggering walk, causing the guards behind us to call a halt until she caught up with Maeve and Cecilia.

"Someone take the dark-haired girl upon his horse so we can reach the castle before midnight," Garreth called.

A guard rode up and plucked her from the ground.

"I would like the same courtesy," Cecilia said. However, when she looked hopefully at the guards around her, no one offered to take her up.

By the time we reached the castle, a good number of the town's people were following us, despite the hour. That Lord Firth lead our procession with the damnable shoe on display had much to do with their curiosity. As did the three bound women in our midst.

Rose waited at the castle gates, as promised, along with two guards, who kept glancing at her.

"That took much longer than I thought it should," she said. "Is it wise to keep a king waiting?"

"Hold your tongue, caster," Lord Firth said as he handed the cushioned shoe to a guard. "We are the King's emissary, and not to be rebuked by the likes of you."

Rose's gaze sharpened on the shoe.

"Why does the King's emissary need a woman's shoe? It hardly becomes your coloring or figure."

I couldn't help the smile that tugged at my lips as Lord Firth sputtered and dismounted.

"Now see here—"

"No, you need to see. I did not make that shoe for you." She looked at me and waved her hand in my direction.

"They were made for her."

The shoe disappeared from the pillow and reappeared on my foot. When I checked the other foot, I found the mate there as well, and my humor faded.

"I don't want the shoes," I said, looking up at her.

"What an ungrateful thing to say. Come along, the King is waiting, and I want to hear the story in full."

She turned and started through the castle gates.

"Stop her," Lord Firth ordered.

The guards who'd stood beside Rose shared a nervous glance.

"We've tried," one said. "But she keeps disappearing before we can touch her."

Rose's chuckle drifted behind her as she started up the castle stairs.

"No man may touch me without my permission," she called.

I was so engrossed in what was happening that I didn't notice Greydon at my side until his hands settled on my waist. He helped me from the horse but didn't immediately release me.

"The shoes look lovely on you," he said quietly.

As I looked up at his handsome, deceptive face, my heart lurched. I'd wanted this man when I'd thought him common and honest like me. He'd broken my trust and my heart by withholding who he was, yet the treacherous organ in my chest still pined for him. If he knew it, would he also seek to use that to his advantage to obtain what he wanted?

"Release me if you want your testicles to remain as they are," I said coolly.

He quickly released me and pivoted so his most prized possession was no longer an easy target.

"This level of aggression is uncalled for," he said, his own anger slipping. "I am not your enemy."

A harsh pull in my stomach and a sudden sickening had me stepping around him.

"That has yet to be determined," I said as I hurried toward Maeve.

The frustrated growl that followed me did nothing to soften my feelings toward him.

Inside the castle, Lord Firth and the guard led us directly to the King's court where numerous people already waited with the exception of Rose. I glanced around the room at those gathered to the right and left of the space, looking for the old woman, but could see her nowhere.

Greydon stepped up beside me and offered his arm. Ignoring it, I followed behind Maeve and my stepsisters, noting the hush that fell over the court as we proceeded forward, toward the King who sat upon his raised throne at the opposite end of the room. An older woman dressed in a plain gown stood on the lowest of the three steps to the King's platform.

"Stop there," she said when we'd crossed half the expanse.

The guard holding Maeve's chains jerked her to a stop. My stepmother studied the older woman as she studied us, her gaze sweeping dismissively over Maeve, Cecilia, and Porcia before finding me. Her expression changed slightly, a combination of joy and sorrow.

"You three stand accused of plotting against the Crown and for the use of magic. How do you plead?" the old woman asked.

"Not guilty, of course," Maeve said. "We've been brought here because one of my daughters has a cut on her heel and the other has a missing toe from birth. That's hardly plotting against the Crown."

The King leaned forward.

"Come now, Maverene," he said. "Admit your guilt. Do you think I don't recognize you? Did you think I would believe this a mere coincidence that you're here now when so much evil has befallen my people? We both know better. I've been long awaiting this moment."

Some of Maeve's mask of innocence dropped.

"As was I, Aftan. Though I imagined our roles reversed. Me on the throne and you in chains, begging for your life."

"Are you saying you plan to beg?"

She smiled serenely.

"I didn't then, and I won't now."

"I thought as much. Your petty acts have—"

"Petty? Petty! You arrogant prick of a man! My actions have never been petty. Unlike yours."

The King's face reddened.

"How you plea matters not. The court finds you guilty, regardless. Silence her and take her away!"

A guard grabbed for her, and I felt a moment of panic.

"Please, Your Majesty," I said, stepping forward. "Silence her if you must, but do not remove her."

Maeve started laughing like a mad woman.

"You see?" she cried. "My daughters are loyal to me."

A guard took a cravat from the nearest man and stuffed it in Maeve's mouth.

"Daughters?" the King said. "These women are not your daughters but your accomplices. You have no daughters."

Hate filled Maeve's gaze, and she screamed something at the King.

"Step forward, Eloise Cartwright," he said, turning his attention to me.

The mention of my name sent a low murmur through the room. I nervously stepped forward a few more feet. Neither he nor the older woman needed to tell me to stop. The slight tug in my stomach told me I'd gone far enough.

"I knew your mother," the king said. "She did a great many selfless acts in the service of this kingdom. Your defense of the vile creature behind you disappoints me. I expected you to be more like your mother."

My temper flared.

"I cannot be any more like her. My every action has been to—"

My throat tightened suddenly, choking the air from my lungs. Gasping, I still tried to force out the words that would convey all that I'd done and endured to attempt to stop Maeve. The spell gripped me harder, closing off my airway, which only increased my need to incriminate Maeve in every way possible. Strangled, pained sounds wheezed from my mouth until I could no longer breathe.

Defeated, I fell to my knees and stopped trying. The ability to breathe slowly returned, and I drew in one ragged breath then another.

A firm hand around my arm helped me stand again when I was ready. I looked up to thank whoever assisted me and met Greydon's tormented gaze.

"Eloise," he said softly. "I'm sorry. I didn't know."

I jerked away from his touch, angry at the whole damn Royal family.

"It is not pity, then, that moved you to speak," the King said.

"No, Sire."

"Perhaps, I can help determine what has transpired," Rose said, emerging from the crowd to the right.

"And you are?" the King asked.

"A simple old woman passing through Towdown on her way to Turre."

"Not simple," Greydon said, stepping toward his father. "Like Maverene, this woman made her presence known shortly after I arrived at the Retreat. That she also uses magic is too coincidental to be ignored."

"Elspeth," the King said, looking at the old woman near his dais. "Do you know her?"

My shocked gaze flew to Elspeth. That was the woman from my mother's letters? The muffled outrage from behind me said that Maeve had recognized the name as well.

Ignoring Maeve, Rose and Elspeth considered one another.

"I do not know her, Sire," Elspeth said.

"Nor do I know you," said Rose. "Should I?"

"No. What is your influence with magic? By blood or nature?"

"Never blood and preferably not nature, though I will when I must."

"What do you use then?" Elspeth asked, her confusion clear.

"Another, more infinitely powerful source that does not require any type of life sacrifice."

The crowd moved restlessly at that confession. I knew very little about the nature of magic with the exception of why all of it was so dangerous. Blood magic was dangerous in that it required a person's life essence, which was what

Maeve had used time and again. Nature magic was the use of the endless energy found in nature. That this woman had found another form was worrisome.

"I require proof of your abilities," Elspeth said. "To assure you do not use blood."

Rose chuckled, and a tingle started in my fingertips, spreading rapidly over the length of my body. Looking down at myself, I watched my gown change from plain to luminescent. From wool to silk. I ran my hand over the ballgown I'd last worn then touched the mask now covering my face. With a good measure of annoyance, I tugged it free and looked at Rose.

"These walls clash with your gown, don't you agree, Eloise?" she said. With a snap of her fingers, the colors on the walls faded from red to a soft blue leafed with golden filigree.

A collective gasp echoed throughout the room.

"I hope you like the colors," Rose said. "As this is no illusion."

Elspeth looked at the King.

"If it were blood magic, we would have felt it."

"Does that sufficiently prove my innocence enough for you to accept my assistance?" Without waiting for anyone's approval, she continued. "Eloise is cursed. There are certain things of which she cannot speak without suffering a great deal of pain. It isn't a magic I can remove. However, I believe Maeve or Maverene, or whatever name she uses, could if she were so inclined."

Maeve made an insistent noise behind her gag.

"Let her speak," the King commanded.

The gag was removed, and she took a moment to wet her lips. Then with great show, she looked around the room before smiling at the King.

"Why should I show pity to the kingdom's apparent favored daughter when none will be shown to me?"

The King's face flushed anew.

"Once again, you are not thinking clearly," he said. "The kingdom may have decided your guilt, but we will not decide your fate. That, I will leave to Eloise. Do you believe she will show you pity when you've shown her none? Perhaps, freeing her now might spare you later."

A hot mixture of feeling flooded me at his words. I'd vowed Maeve would pay for all that I'd suffered, and now it would be within my power to see it done.

Maeve's gaze shifted to me. She smiled slightly and nodded her head at me in acknowledgement.

"Eloise is far too much like me, filled with anger and loathing, to show any pity now."

Her words struck me like a knife because I realized how true they were. I wanted to be nothing like Maeve.

"Then, you shall continue to enjoy the gag," the King said.

Maeve struggled but was gagged as ordered.

Once the room quieted, Rose circled me.

"Speak what you can," she said. "Maeve cursed you because she sought to keep you silent about something.

Most likely her actions. Tell me what has happened to you and to the kingdom since she arrived."

She wasn't asking what Maeve had done or that I implicate Maeve in any way. She was asking me to relate events. I opened my mouth and tentatively spoke the first words.

"My sister left in the middle of the night." Admitting that truth, something that I'd already shared, was easy. The next was harder. "Our house maids died." My chest tightened as I recalled their shriveled forms. They were the first of many. But not all by Maeve's hand. Tears clogged my throat when I thought of Hugh.

"Our manservant died, too." The words began to spill from me. "As did many men in town. Many became ill. A small child died horribly. I walked the length of Towdown naked and covered in ash, vomiting. People threw rocks at me, among other things. One person showed pity. He was blinded. I was beaten. Almost raped. Starved. Chained."

"Stop." Greydon's broken plea pulled me from the memories.

Angry, I looked up at him.

"Why? Does your ignorance absolve you of any fault for what I've suffered? For what others have suffered while the Royal family stayed safely hidden away? Is it not your games for power and control that caused this?"

There was a rustle of noise from the front of the room, and when I looked, I saw the King descending the steps of his platform.

"Allow me to explain why the suffering was necessary," he said. "Years ago, when I was closer to Greydon's age, my father tasked me to find a suitable bride. He wanted me to choose a maiden from our kingdom rather than attempt to strike alliances with others. I toured the land, looking for a maiden who would not only capture my heart but make a suitable queen.

"I thought I found such a maiden in Maverene. She was fair to look upon and kind and just in her dealings with others. Or so I thought. It wasn't until she was faced with a test of fertility that her true nature was revealed. I released her, thinking her vehement cries for retribution no more than a woman's wounded pride."

Maeve made loud sounds from behind her gag, but the King ignored her.

"Then I found Sevil," he said. "She was everything Maverene was not and became a true queen, who ruled fairly and justly at my side. However, a few years after we'd wed, a plague befell our kingdom. It was unnatural in its form and swiftness."

I recalled the beast Garreth had shown me in the Royal Retreat's trophy room and shivered.

"Your mother helped stop the spread, and for a few months, we found peace once more. But Sevil and I knew it was nothing more than a trick. An attempt to lull us. And because of that, we kept a precious secret. That of Sevil's second pregnancy. However, such a thing is impossible to keep truly secret. During the final weeks of Sevil's seclusion, Maverene learned of it and began to attack the child while it still grew within Sevil. Only the amulet my wife wore kept the babe safe."

The King remained silent for a long moment.

"The man you know as Prince Greydon is actually Prince Garreth, my second son. He was taken away by a trusted friend the moment of his birth. To keep him safe, we let the kingdom believe he was dead while we searched for Maverene. Too often, Elspeth would draw close to finding Maverene only to have her disappear again."

"Meanwhile, my sons grew, and I aged. Time waits for no man, and I was forced to keep the secret of my second son's existence and send my first born to find a suitable bride. I had hoped Maverene had set aside her anger after so many years. However, when Prince Greydon's wife died enroute to the castle, I knew the kingdom was not yet safe, and I needed to draw out the evil stalking us."

"The decisions made were never meant to retain power or control but to protect the kingdom from one who sought to hurt it. For, it was rarely the Royal family who suffered but our people."

The heavy weight that had formed inside of me the moment I learned Kaven's true identity remained firmly in place. Yet, some of the anger lifted. Maeve had never sought to hurt the people but the King, through his people. And, after living with her for so long, I knew that had the King given up his throne or taken her to be his wife, the same misery would have still befallen the kingdom. That was Maeve's nature. The King had made the best choice he had available to him. Hadn't I done the same? Hadn't those choices resulted in other people's misery? I thought of Mother, Judith, Anne, Hugh, the small child, and Alfie. If I didn't hold the blame for their treatment, was it fair to expect the King to hold the blame for mine.

"Thank you for telling me, Sire," I said.

The King nodded and squeezed my arm compassionately.

"The time for secrecy is at an end. I do not need you to speak against Maverene for me to know her guilt. You need only to speak her punishment."

An involuntary shiver ran through me as I was consumed by a severe chill followed by an uncomfortable heat. Inhaling sharply, I looked to Rose, who smiled slightly. Her words from when we sat in the kitchen of the Brazen Belle came back to me.

I smiled in return and turned to look at the gagged woman who had destroyed my life.

For the first time in months, I spoke freely.

"Maeve has killed men, women, and children. I would say let her suffer those travesties. Shave her head, blind her, beat her, strip her bare, and let her walk the streets so the people she has caused untold suffering can judge her as they will."

King Aftan nodded.

"A just ruling. So it shall be. Take Maverene away."

The guards began to drag her away, her cries of anger

muted by the gag. The tug in my middle had me stumbling toward her.

"Wait," I called. "She cannot yet leave me. Nor I, her. If we're separated, I will suffer sickness unlike anything I've felt before."

"Was it cast after my spell of protection?"

I nodded, and Rose came to me, setting her hand on my heart and my head.

"Good. That means it won't have rooted as deeply as the first spell." She remained quiet for a moment then made a satisfied sound. "Just as I thought."

Another wave, hot and cold, spread throughout my body.

"Having them removed is much more pleasant that receiving them, isn't it?" Rose asked.

"It is. Thank you."

"You can remove Maverene," Rose said. "Eloise will be fine."

The guard looked at the King, who nodded his agreement, and I watched the men drag Maeve away, feeling true freedom.

"The hour grows late, and I have no knowledge of the two remaining women," the King said. "Let them share the same fate as the woman they chose to call mother."

"Wait," Cecilia cried. "Like Eloise, we were nothing more than pawns in Maverene's pursuit of power. Tell them, Eloise. Tell them we had no choice just like when you killed your lover, Hugh."

Anger blinded me. With a cry, I flew at her. She stepped behind her guard and, with an evil smile, knocked him forward as he drew his sword for her.

The honed edge of the blade flashed in the candle light as he stumbled toward me.

CHAPTER SEVENTEEN

STRONG ARMS CIRCLED MY WAIST AND SPUN ME ABOUT, sparing me from the blade but also keeping me from my target. I struggled against the firm hold as I was surrounded by guards. Instead of putting me in chains, they faced outward, shielding my struggle from the people gathered.

"He wasn't a lover but someone I loved," I yelled. "And the fault of his death lies on you and the evil bitch you call mother."

"Settle yourself," Greydon whispered in my ear. "Don't allow her to cause you further suffering. You're free from their will and better than they are in every way."

I inhaled deeply and calmed myself.

"Release me." He did so reluctantly, and the guards retreated, showing the two men who now held Cecilia tightly.

She watched me with a malicious glint in her eyes. Even caught and sentenced for treason, there was no remorse within her.

"At every turn, I watched your delight as others have suffered," I said.

"And you helped in that suffering," she replied. "You sat at the same table. You put your safety before the safety of others. How are we any different? Why should I be punished when you walk free?"

A murmur rose in the court.

"Because, however small my actions, they were always to fight against the outcome you and Maeve wanted. You wanted to be queen, Cecilia, for you, not for Maeve. And if you'd wed Garreth as you'd planned, everyone would have suffered."

"Lies," she hissed. "You have no proof."

"You wanted to break his charm of protection, and I pushed him out of the way."

"That was your attempt to break it," she said, lying.

"You poisoned his drink so he couldn't walk me home."

I looked at Porcia, who had remained subdued since entering the court.

"Do I speak the truth?"

"You do," she said softly. "Our actions brought unspeakable pain, suffering, and death to countless people here and across this kingdom. Any participation forced upon you was under great duress."

"Traitor," Cecilia said harshly.

"Your sentence, Eloise?" the King asked.

"Shave Cecilia's head, beat her, starve her, and brand her forehead so everyone knows her as a traitor to the Crown. But do not blind her. Let her witness every look of revulsion and know what it is to be alone in this world."

The guards dragged her away as she screeched words of revenge at me.

"And the other?" the King asked.

I looked at Porcia, who met my gaze steadily. The lack of hatred in her eyes gave me pause.

"How does a barren woman come to have two daughters?" I asked.

"She steals them. The ones who learn their lessons quickly live to learn more. The ones who don't...well, you saw what happens."

"She did to you and Cecilia what she did to me?"

"Not to Cecilia. Cecilia embraced all that Maeve was and all that she wanted, no matter what the cost."

"And you?"

"I could never forget my real mother's face," she said without malice. "Or what she would think of the monster I'd become."

"A monster you chose to become."

"Imagine not a few weeks of failed lessons but years. Cecilia and I weren't her only daughters. There were many who never learned their lessons. I learned from their mistakes and many of my own. I told you to learn quickly because I knew how it would progress. Magic can smooth away scars, so I bear no marks of what I endured. But, they were lessons I will never forget and would do anything never to repeat. I've suffered more than one person should and caused equal suffering in turn to spare myself."

I didn't like Porcia. However, I did understand what she was saying. She'd done what she must to survive. I hadn't had to endure years of Maeve's manipulations. If I had, would I have deaths on my conscious, too?

"I've done vile things, and I regret those actions more than you know," she continued. "I cannot change the past. Yet, I beg the court for mercy."

"You presume to ask for mercy after all the lives you've allowed Maeve to take?" the King said with outrage.

"Allowed? You had the support of an entire kingdom yet could not stop her, Your Majesty. I had no real power to stand against her and was spelled to prevent speaking against her until my actions had damned me just as certainly as they had her. It was never a question of allowing anything."

"It was survival," I said.

She nodded.

"All I request is a quick death. I'm tired and wish for this wretched excuse for a life to be over."

Had I not thought the same thing only weeks into my life with Maeve? Had I not sat on the cliff and considered jumping? I thought of all that I suffered since her arrival then tried to imagine years of it. I'd witnessed for myself how Maeve would lash out at the two. How Porcia had been her least favorite by far.

"A quick death would be a mercy," I agreed. "One I cannot justly give. Yet, having experienced Maeve's reeducation, I find I cannot fault you for self-preservation. It is what anyone would do."

"You did not," she said. "You continued to defy her."

"I defied her at great risk to Kellen's safety. My defiance cost others their lives. I once told someone that a king's life should hold no more value than a common man's life. I still believe that to be true. Thus, I cannot now say your life is less precious because of the circumstances you were forced into. Yet, you are not without guilt or cruelty.

"You will not be marked or mistreated. You will find menial employment in a bakery and work every day to serve the people who suffered because of your compliancy."

Porcia looked to the King, her expression showing neither relief nor fear. Only acceptance.

"Put her in the dungeon with the others," the King ordered. "She will watch their fates before seeking her own."

While the guard led Porcia away, the King turned to look at Rose.

"The use of magic in this kingdom is forbidden. For your service this night, I will suspend judgement against your crimes and suggest that you leave for Turre immediately."

"I understand, Sire. One can never be too watchful of the temerity of those with power."

She chuckled and disappeared. For a moment, the King just stared at the spot she'd been. Then, he turned to me and offered his arm.

"It's time for me to retire. Walk with me."

Setting my hand lightly on his sleeve, I left the whispering court and listened to several sets of footsteps echo behind us.

"Greydon has told me of his affection for you," the King said when we reached the private hallway that led to the rooms I'd seen the night of the last ball. "And his offer for your hand and of your recent rejection of that offer. I ask you to reconsider."

"My life has changed so rapidly, and there is too much yet unsaid to give a fair and honest answer. But, I can promise I no longer want to push either of your sons from the highest turret."

He chuckled.

"Your mother was an honest woman as well. We will speak of this again tomorrow. Until then, you'll be our guest."

The thought of spending the night here, so close to Greydon, upset me because I knew what would happen. He would seek me out. He would attempt to sway me with his words and touch. I wouldn't be forced to make a decision I was not yet ready to make.

"Forgive me, Sire, but I would prefer to go home. There's much I must set to rights."

"Oh?"

"The last two maids she brought to the house are in the attic. Dead. And Seth is still there. Though he is not guilty of murder, I do not trust him. There is little left of my mother and father, but I would like to keep what there is."

"I understand. However, I cannot let you go alone."

"I will take her home, Father," Greydon said from behind me.

"A guard or two will be fine," I said, quickly.

The King smiled.

"I think some time to discuss those unsaid things might be just what is needed before we speak again tomorrow. Don't you agree?" He didn't wait for my answer before looking beyond me. "Now that I've made known who you truly are, the kingdom will be watching. Take an escort and a chaperone."

"Yes, Father."

The King released my hand.

"Go. Garreth, you will attend me."

I stepped aside and allowed Garreth to pass me. Left alone with Greydon, I finally turned to look at him fully.

"Will you tell me everything?" he asked softly. "From the beginning?"

It was the last thing I'd expected him to say and the one thing that stalled my anger.

"It's not pleasant," I said.

"That's precisely why I need to hear it. I was so blinded by what my family was facing that I didn't know the full extent of what you were facing."

"You never suspected it was Maeve?"

He paused and offered me his arm, which I took.

"I began suspecting Maeve when I met Cecilia and she introduced herself as your sister. She said 'Mama' sent her to find you. I found it odd that after hearing you state your father's love for your mother, he would re-wed so quickly. However, as I asked questions during our encounters after that, you seemed ignorant of who Maeve might be. I never thought she was hurting you. You were her reason for maintaining a presence there. If all your family had gone missing, it would have been obvious."

Her need to keep me alive became so much clearer.

"Tell me what really happened," he said again.

As he led me to the stables, waited for our shared mount, and then started home, I related my sorrowful tale, beginning with the gift that I thought was from my father. The guards trailed in our wake, a discreet distance away.

I told Greydon how I'd suspected him because of the boy's cap. He said little as I spoke of Judith and Anne's deaths, Hugh's odd devotion to Maeve, or the first conversation I had with Rose about magic. I relived that moment of fear when I explained how I'd witnessed Maeve draining Hugh and how I'd tried to run.

Greydon's arms tightened around me as I continued through my beatings and the times spent chained to the hearth. It hurt to speak of Kellen and Maeve's use of the huntsman to keep me in line.

"I didn't know the depth of her depravity until her daughters arrived with her mirror," I said.

I told him of the dinners. Of how Maeve had used Heather and Catherine and drained the men. Of how she'd tried to use the mirror to find him, and used it to spy on Kellen and others in the court, instead.

Relaying the full tale took its toll on me. I relived every horrific moment. Every terrible death. When I needed to stop and grieve for a moment, he held me in silence. The quiet of the night and the gentle sway of the horse helped soothe me as well.

By the time we reached the road to the Royal Retreat, I'd told him everything. I felt lighter and freer for it.

"Forgive me, Eloise. In my self-centered need for revenge, I was blind to your suffering. I will never be able to forgive myself."

I twisted in his lap to look up at him.

"Don't be foolish. I purposely misled you so you wouldn't see the truth. It was only your ignorance and the Prince's favor that kept you safe. You wouldn't be here now if not for both. She threatened your safety many times to keep me in line."

"I am to just accept that you were beaten, chained, and taught how to act as a whore so I could remain safe?"

"No, you have a choice. You can dwell on what's happened and let your hate and anger destroy any chance of future happiness, or you can find a way to accept it and move forward to make a better, happier life for yourself."

He was silent as we started up the path to my home.

"I cannot tell you what to choose," I added. "But I will tell you what I choose. Tomorrow, I will watch Maeve suffer every torment she inflicted upon me, and I will pity her inability to let go of the past hate and anger that drove her to that point. Then, I will walk away and never think of her again."

He pressed a kiss to my temple and brought the horse to a halt in the yard.

"There should be enough room in the stable for the horses," I said. "If not, you can put them in with the pig. He won't bother them."

"With your permission, I'll dismiss your groomsman on your behalf, too," Greydon said, helping me down.

"Please do. When you're done, come inside. There are plenty of rooms and beds in the attic to accommodate everyone."

"I'll come in," Greydon said. "However, the guards will make use of the stables and keep watch out here."

I didn't comment about our lack of chaperone. After all, it was a moot point. My innocence was long since gone in many ways.

Instead, I nodded and let myself inside. The house echoed its silence around me as I crossed the entry, the dying fire from the sitting room barely casting any light. Upstairs, I went to the room that used to belong to Kellen and me and opened the door. Porcia had removed Kellen's bed but had kept much of the room the same, unlike Cecilia with Father's room.

Lighting a candle, I looked at the dress lying over the back of the chair beside the wardrobe. It was one of my old dresses. Cecilia had taken a knife to it, rending it down the middle from neckline to hem. There were other cuts in it too, making it irreparable. I wondered why Porcia had even kept it. Balling it up, I turned to leave the room, intending to gather all of their clothes to take into town with me the next day.

However, I froze at the sight of Seth in the doorway.

"I thought you might be the only one to return," he said.

"An obvious conclusion since the others were led away in chains."

"A pity for sure. I've never been so thoroughly fucked before coming here. Maeve rode me hard daily. I can still feel her on me, in me, calling to me." He looked at the window, in the direction of the castle. "I know right where she is. I can feel it." He smiled and looked at me.

"But the spell she kept trying to cast on me didn't quite take, I think, because I couldn't stop seeing you, bathed in moonlight as you washed in the horse trough."

He took a step toward me.

"I want to make you scream," he said. "I want to hear you moan my name as you ride me like she did."

I felt no fear as he approached me.

"Will you force me?" I asked.

He chuckled.

"I don't mind a bit of a struggle."

"I do," I said as he stopped before me. I could smell his sweat and the faint odor of horse.

"Do you know what happened to the last groomsman? The one you replaced? I killed him for trying to force himself on me."

Seth grinned.

"You're just building the anticipation, luv."

"Allow me to kill it," Greydon said from behind him.

Seth jerked and grunted, the smile fading from his lips. He pivoted slowly to face Greydon, and I saw the knife sticking out from Seth's back.

"Miss Cartwright planned to dismiss you," Greydon said. "After your compliancy with what has transpired here, I'm not quite so benevolent."

Seth slumped to his knees and looked up at me, coughing on his blood. I felt no pity for him.

"You should have left when you had the chance," I said.

As he fell to the floor, I looked at Greydon.

"Can you have the guards remove him as well as the maids upstairs? We can use the wagon to take them to town so their families can claim them."

"Of course." He studied me. "Are you all right?"

"No. But I will be."

He nodded and left the room. I stepped over Seth and began removing any hint of Maeve, Cecilia, and Porcia's presence in my home. It wasn't until sunup that the house once again looked like it had before my mother's death.

"Thank you," I said to the weary guards as they went downstairs.

"We will rest for two hours then must leave for the castle," Greydon said.

"Yes, Sire," the lead guard said with a bow before closing the front door.

Greydon turned to me and took my hand.

"Where are we going?"

"To bed."

I briefly considered pulling my hand from his as he led me to my mother's room, but I was too tired and didn't want to be alone. For all of my thoughts of accepting the past, the things that happened in this house still echoed in my mind. I couldn't stop seeing Maeve with Hugh in my mother's room.

Greydon seemed to know it too for he pulled me into his arms and tucked me close against his chest as we lay fully dressed on top of the covers.

"What was your mother like?"

I smiled slightly and shared my memories of her until I fell asleep.

"CAN I interest you in a citrus tart, miss?" a server asked.

"I couldn't eat another bite if I wanted to," I said with a kind smile.

The dress I wore was impressive and well corseted. One of the many surprises that had greeted me since waking in an abundantly feathered bed at the castle. That I'd slept through leaving the estate, the carriage ride here, and being carried inside still amazed me.

The server took away my plate, and I looked at the table's three other occupants.

"I apologize for sleeping so late," I said to the King.

"Nonsense. Greydon told me all that you accomplished when you returned. And all that you had endured since your mother's death. I'm truly sorry, Eloise. For her death and for all that you suffered. We are forever in your debt as we were in hers."

"As I told Greydon, the past is passed."

"Almost. There are a few more things yet to attend to."

He stood and offered his arm.

"If you will allow me to walk with you," he said.

"Of course, Your Majesty."

"Ah, yes," he said, setting his hand over mine and leading me from the room. "Your Majesty seems too formal for a new daughter, don't you agree? We must decide on a new title."

"Shouldn't that wait until I agree to Greydon's proposal?"

"Do you love the boy?"

"The boy is right here," Greydon said dryly from behind us.

"Your Majesty, considering all that's happened because of Maeve with Sevil and my mother...doesn't it prove that love is not enough?"

"Just the opposite," he said. "If not for the love Sevil bore for her family and for the love your mother bore for you and Sevil, the kingdom would have fallen long ago." He stopped walking to look me in the eye. "Above all else, the future queen needs to feel a great deal of love for her future king and for her future people. I think you will do well in both."

Trumpets blasted outside the main doors, and the King heaved a sigh.

"Duty demands our attention, and I can see you need more time to consider Greydon's proposal. We will speak of this later."

As we started forward once more, I glanced back at Greydon. His deep blue gaze caught and held mine, and his promise that I would be his echoed in my mind.

CHAPTER EIGHTEEN

THE FOUR OF US, FOLLOWED BY THE KING'S ADVISORS,
continued down the steps toward the gate. Once there, we
climbed the stairs to watch the proceedings from the top of
the walls surrounding the castle.

"Good people of Drisdall," the King called. "This is a
day for celebration. Before you stand the condemned. They
are responsible for tormenting our kingdom with their evil
magic. Their reign of terror is at an end, and Drisdall is
once again the safe home you knew and loved."

The King nodded to a man below, who began listing
Maeve's crimes as she was brought forward. The list of
what she'd done was horrific, but so were her injuries. She
could barely walk. Bruises covered her body, and blood
covered her face. As I'd ordered, she'd been blinded and
shaved.

As I watched, the hate I felt toward her bled out from the well in which I'd kept it imprisoned for so long.

"Maeve Grimmoire confessed to her crimes and has been sentenced to suffer as we have suffered," the King said. "Her life, what is left of it, is her own when she reaches the docks. Any who choose to take pity on her there, may."

The people jeered and threw rocks at her as she stumbled forward. One hit her square in the hip and knocked her to the ground before she had gone very far. And, I felt pity as she lay there, struggling to get up, and wondered whether she would have been able to let go of her hate and anger for the King if she would have known her fate. I doubted it.

Once Maeve stopped moving, Cecilia was brought forward, and her crimes were listed as well. She sobbed and looked at the crowd before her as they reacted to her wrongdoings. She was no better than her mother, and she saw it as she looked for any mercy within the throng. Like Maeve, she was beaten and shaven but also branded.

"Cecilia Grimmoire confessed to her crimes and has been sentenced to endure the same suffering as those she tormented. Her life, what is left of it, is her own when she reaches the docks."

Being able to see, Cecilia ran forward, covering her head with her arms. She didn't pause when she reached Maeve's still form but continued down the road as rocks pelted her. I knew she would make it to the docks.

"Have I made a mistake?" I asked the King. "Will she, like Maverene, cause the kingdom grief in the years to come?"

"The old woman who was here yesterday did something so they can never use magic again without great pain and suffering."

"Her life will not be easy, then," I said, relieved that Rose had done such a thing.

"And that is why your punishment is just," the King answered.

Porcia was brought forward, and her crimes listed.

"Porcia, originally of the northern Devenire's, was taken from her family at a young age and forced to do Maeve's will or suffer Maeve's cruelty. She did not seek power; she sought only to survive. While we do not find her innocent, we also cannot condemn her to the extent we have condemned the first two women."

The crowd remained quiet as the King asked for a baker willing to employ her at a fair wage to step forward. Porcia looked at the people, her fear openly displayed on her face.

"I will take her on," a young man said, stepping forward. "However, I cannot offer a fair wage. My business is new, and there is no profit for pay. I can offer a room and two meals a day, instead."

The King looked at Porcia.

"She will accept those conditions."

Porcia left with the man, disappearing into the crowd.

"To celebrate our freedom and the return of my youngest son, Prince Garreth, we will have another ball in one week's time. All will be invited."

With a wave, the King started down the steps, leaving Greydon to escort me.

"Would you walk with me in the private gardens?" he asked when we reached the main hall.

"Of course."

He led me through the court, which was already filling with people, and out to the private gardens. We walked in silence for several minutes.

"My full name is Greydon Perth Kaven Drisdall. The day Garreth was born will never leave me. I remember the terror of losing my mother and looking at the small baby who caused it. I held him to blame. Then, he was gone, too, and my father mourned deeply. I didn't fully understand the significance of what had happened that day until years later when my father told me I, too, needed to leave and gave me a task. Protect my brother. By then, I was old enough to understand that he wasn't to blame for our mother's death.

"While the kingdom thought I left often for diplomatic journeys, I was with my brother, teaching him about our family and how to be a prince."

"How old were you when you and your brother first met?"

"I was sixteen, and he was eleven. Elspeth raised him as

her own and only told him of his true heritage the eve before I arrived."

"I can't imagine the shock of learning such a thing."

"He was angry the truth had been kept from him. That he'd been lied to for so long even if it was to keep him safe. In time, he forgave Elspeth and Father."

He stopped walking and faced me.

"And, in time, I hope you can forgive me."

"I understand why you said nothing about who you really were. And I am not angry. Not anymore. No matter what name you used, you never lied about your intentions, for here you stand, still determined to make me yours."

"And yet, you're still reluctant. Why?"

"I was content with the idea of wedding a servant. Of a simple life. Then, I was willing to sacrifice that dream to save the kingdom from whatever fate Maeve had planned for it. But I never planned to stay wed to the Prince. That's why I asked you to wait for me in the woods."

"You thought he would what? Set you aside after discovering you were no longer innocent?"

"That was my hope."

"So it isn't me you oppose but truly what I am?"

I didn't answer him.

He studied me for several long moments, his expression giving nothing away.

"When I met Idina, my first wife, she was everything my father told me a wife should be. Graceful, fair of face, soft spoken. I wed her because she was kind and compassionate. I knew she would become a queen who would never put her needs before the needs of the people of Drisdall. But she never made my heart race with a word or a look. Nor did she challenge my thoughts or choices. She didn't make me a better man like you do."

He gently touched my cheek.

"I never felt for her as I feel for you. You say you cannot accept what I am, and I say I cannot accept a life without you. Whatever it is you fear when you think of yourself as my wife, set it aside. I swear to you, if you agree to wed me, I will never give you cause to regret it."

I turned my head and kissed his palm.

"And I give you the same answer I gave your father. I need time. Reacting rashly to the choices life presents me has gotten me into more trouble than not. Whatever decision I make, I want to ensure it will be the best for everyone."

Frustration crept into his gaze.

"Please, Greydon. Is it not enough that I'm here? Can you not give me some time to let the events of these past months settle in my mind?"

He exhaled slowly.

"I apologize for pressing you. Would you like to sit and watch the water for a bit? I can fetch us something to drink."

"Thank you."

I settled on the stone bench as he left and listened to the burble of water as it ran over the rocks. Taking a slow, deep breath, I did as I said I would and let the reality of the current moment settle in my mind. Maeve was gone. Dead in the street by the people she sought to subjugate. I wondered if she had wanted to be queen before she met Aftan.

"Why do you hesitate to grab the future waiting for you?" Rose asked from beside me, startling me from my thoughts.

"How do you do that?"

"Magic, of course." She chuckled. "Are you going to tell me why you are refusing what so many would not hesitate to accept?"

"I never wanted to be queen. And certainly not someone's wife."

"And now?"

"I need to find my sister, Kellen. She ran into the Dark Forest."

"You know you cannot find her alone. Ask for Prince Greydon's help, and he will give it without condition. However, the need to find your sister isn't the reason you're not giving that man the answer he so desperately seeks. Is he cruel?"

"Not unless necessary."

"Do you find him unpleasant to look upon?"

"I very much like looking at him."

Rose harrumphed.

"Then it is a good thing that I asked for two small favors in return for helping you instead of one."

I'd forgotten about her stipulation and regarded her now with growing concern.

"And what two favors do you ask of me?"

"First is that you wed Prince Greydon."

"Why?"

"Because this kingdom is yet in need of you."

"But I have no desire to rule over anyone."

"Then don't. Serve the people. See to their welfare as only a queen can. Continue to protect them as you have."

Having been under Maeve's influence, my greatest fear in accepting Greydon's proposal had been that I would be expected to be cold and use the people to serve my needs, whatever they might be. But hearing Rose's words helped me start to see my error in how I thought of those with titles and wealth.

"And your second favor?"

"For some, magic is as natural as breathing. Is it fair or just for a queen to ask her subjects to cease breathing because one of the subjects might have wicked intentions?"

"I see." I looked out over the green lawn for a moment. "I will do as you ask."

"Good." She started to stand.

"You're leaving?"

"Indeed. If you recall, I was traveling to the Kingdom of Turre with my pig when I met you."

"Who is the pig?" I asked.

"That's a Beastly Tale better left for another time. But

rest assured, I am not Maeve. I don't curse idly or for my own benefit."

I studied her for a moment, then nodded. Even if I doubted her word, which I didn't, there would have been little I could have done about it.

"I know I have no right to ask this, but on your way to Turre, would you be willing to stop at a cabin in the Dark Forest? Maeve used an apple to curse my sister, and I'm worried that even the King's guards might not be able to help her."

Rose patted my hand.

"I will check on her on my way to Adele."

"The place with the white towers?" I asked, remembering our very first conversation.

"That's right. Rule well, Eloise. Be a fair and just queen, and don't forget your promise."

When Greydon returned with our drinks, Rose had vanished into air.

"I have news," he said, sitting beside me.

"Oh?"

"I've told my father I have no wish to be King and asked that he name Garreth the first in line. He asked for some time to consider my request, but I know he will agree."

I stared at him in surprise. When I told Greydon I needed time and admitted why, I had never even considered he would abdicate. That he was willing to do so...

My throat tightened for what I felt for the man beside me.

"It won't change who I am," he continued, looking at me earnestly, "but perhaps it will—"

I grabbed the front of his jacket and pulled him down for a kiss. After a moment, I heard the glasses fall to the lawn and felt his arms encircle me. He deepened the kiss before breaking away.

"Does that mean you accept?"

"Yes, but only if you tell your father you're a fool for saying you'd give up your crown for a woman."

"Never. I would do anything to have you, Eloise. When are you going to understand that?"

I smiled up at the man who had stolen my heart.

"I think I'm beginning to understand that now. I'll wed you, Greydon. And, together we will serve and protect the people of this kingdom."

He swept me up into his arms and gave a whoop of joy as he spun me around.

I was pleading for mercy moments later. Instead of placing me on my feet, he continued to carry me as he strode toward the castle.

"I can walk."

"You can also run, and I'm not going to risk that. Not now that you've agreed."

He stopped moving to kiss me soundly. Garreth's raucous cheering echoed for a moment before I lost myself to the feel of Greydon.

CHAPTER NINETEEN

I WALKED THE FAMILIAR PATH TO MY MOTHER'S GRAVE AND listened to the bird song. As it always did when I was in the woods, the volume of the animals increased. I'd learned it wasn't only here they did that but in the castle gardens as well. In the days since agreeing to wed Greydon, he'd continued to use their clamor to find me.

Smiling softly at the thought of him, I entered the charred clearing and sat on the undamaged bench Hugh had made for us. It still hurt to think of him. I doubted that would ever stop.

"There's so much you probably already know," I began. "The necklace wasn't from Father but from the caster you tried to stop from hurting the queen and her unborn babe so long ago. Father didn't leave us willingly. He was cursed, like I was. Like Kellen is." I stopped for a moment, trying to control my fear for my twin. "I don't want you to worry about us, though. We're safe now. Maeve is gone. Dead by my sentencing. It was a harsh punishment. She was made to endure much of the suffering she'd brought to others."

I paused, recalling the scene and my pity for her.

"King Aftan said it wasn't jealousy that brought all of this about but her need for power. I think it was something more. I lived with her and saw her twisted form of love. What kind of family could create such a creature?"

Inhaling deeply, I set thoughts of Maeve aside as I'd promised myself I would do.

"I'm grateful that I had you and Kellen and Father and miss you all terribly. Judith and Anne are dead. Anne's Mother and cousin, too. As is Hugh." I brushed my hand against the wood, letting the grief out. Tears, long overdue, coursed down my cheeks. I didn't tell Mother how he'd tried to hurt me or how I'd needed to kill him in the end.

"So much loss," I managed through my tears. "No one person should have to bear so much loss in such a short time." I let out a shaky exhale.

"Greydon is doing everything he can to help me forget. But, he doesn't understand that some things will never be forgotten. At night, I relive much of what has happened. I wake shaking and cold. He's there to comfort me and redoubles his efforts to help me forget." I wiped at my warming cheeks as I recalled last night's efforts. "He's wonderful, Mother, and I know you would approve. Not for his position or title but for who he is as a man."

"We're to be wed in two weeks' time. The King wanted

us to wed sooner, but I wanted to give enough time for the men he sent after Kellen to return with her." Worry ate at my mind once more. "She ran before the worst of it, but I don't think she was fully spared. I don't know what's befallen her. When Maeve returned from delivering the cursed apple, she said that Kellen was alive but that no prince would ever have her. But I will continue to love her no matter what's befallen her. The King's Guard will also search for Father, though the King warned me not to hold too much hope."

I sighed.

"There's a very likely chance that I will wed with no family in attendance. I will have a friend there, though. Well, of a sort. Remember the boy I hit in the head with the pan? The very one who I once spit a mouthful of ale at? He showed me kindness when I most needed it and paid for it with his eyes."

My tears started anew as I thought of Alfie's terror when I'd finally found him again. He was still shaken and startled easily at anyone's approach.

"I swore I would repay his kindness, and I have. There was a girl he fancied. I spoke to her on his behalf and explained what had happened. She's good for him and to him. With her, he's recovering and learning what it means to live with what's happened."

Much like me, I thought.

"They're to be wed soon. The celebration will happen just outside the castle gates. The King's generosity is vast.

Something I wouldn't have guessed. I have a personal seamstress now. A young girl from a poor family. You would like her. She suggested I wear wool and cotton when all the others brought me silks and lace. Her reason was because I didn't look the pampered type. I looked like I was more likely to climb a tree." I laughed lightly. "She'll suit me well."

I sat for a while, feeling the sun on my face and listening to the bird song before I stood and gazed at the barren patch of earth that had once been covered by the pear tree, grass, and blooms.

"I snuck away from the castle and need to return before my absence is noted. But don't worry. I'll be back to plant another tree, and I'll visit often to watch it grow. Thank you for everything you did, Mother. I know you're still watching over me. Watch over Kellen, too. Bring her home to me if you can."

With an ache in my chest, I walked away from the grave. The animals continued to sing to me until the path opened to the yard. There, a semi-familiar face waited. Elspeth.

I crossed the quiet yard to join her by the front door.

"How did you know I would be here?"

She smiled and followed me toward the door.

"A location spell."

Horror filled me, and I set my hand on the door to steady myself. It took a moment for me to look back at Elspeth.

"Whatever you think I've done terrifies you," she said, pity filling her expression. "Will you tell me what it is before you set your mind against me?"

"Maeve did a location spell. It cost a child its life." The image of the small heart in a bowl flashed in my mind again. It was one of the many moments I relived at night.

Elspeth's expression turned to sorrow.

"That's because Maeve gained her power through blood magic, a perverted form of the magic casters are born with. Magic isn't in blood but in the manipulation of the life energies around us. It's meant to be natural. A balanced existence. As we stand here, I can feel the trees, the birds, and the grass around us. If I needed, I could draw some of that energy. However, just enough to manipulate but not enough to cause harm to that from which I drew."

"Can you feel my energy?"

"I can. Though I would never use the energy from a living creature, unless I had no choice. It can be dangerous."

"You're like Rose, then?"

Elspeth gave a half-laugh.

"Only in the most basic sense. Her abilities extend far beyond mine. Maybe even beyond the abilities of the casters who created the Dark Forest."

"Is she dangerous?"

Elspeth considered me for a moment.

"Anyone with power has the capacity to be dangerous.

It's our actions that determine our character and intent. Do you believe Rose is dangerous?"

Instead of answering, I opened the door to my old home and gestured for Elspeth to enter. There was a chill in the air, and a slight mustiness had settled in from disuse. Moving to the sitting room, I set about building a small fire even though I didn't plan on staying long.

"Rose helped me in exchange for two promises," I said when I finished.

Elspeth was seated in Kellen's chair, which once again faced Mother's lounge.

"Oh? And what did she ask of you?"

"The first one was easy. She wanted me to wed Greydon." I sat in my chair and gazed out the window.

"You didn't want to marry him?"

"I wanted to marry Kaven, the man I knew, not the Crown Prince who will someday be King."

When I looked at Elspeth to see what she thought of that, humor lit her gaze.

"And the second promise?" she asked.

"She wants the ban against magic lifted."

The humor left Elspeth's expression.

"Why?"

"Because it's wrong. Magic is a part of our world. By forbidding those with the ability from using it, King Aftan is creating resentment and fear. As you said, anyone with power has the capacity to be dangerous. That applies to people who have magic and those who don't. It's not the magic that makes a person evil but how they use it."

"You are your mother's daughter," Elspeth said. "She often said the same thing to me about magic and about those with wealth. She didn't want to marry a titled man, either. Instead, she married your father, a merchant."

"You knew her well?" I asked, studying the old woman.

"Since she was as tall as my knee. Her mother would often come to me for potions to help with fertility. When they didn't work, Lady Thoning stopped coming but not Margaret." A smile lifted Elspeth's lips. "She was trouble in a good way. A restless spirit who wasn't content with the injustices in our world."

Elspeth sighed and reached out for my hand, which I reluctantly gave.

"I loved your mother as my own. Everything that befell her broke my heart. I'm so sorry she's gone." She gave my hand a light squeeze and released me.

"I read your letters to her," I said.

She shook her head.

"I warned her to burn them. It was dangerous to keep them."

"I'm glad she did. They serve as proof that you're telling the truth. Why did you leave?"

"To protect your mother, her new twins, and Queen Sevil's babe."

"Garreth?"

"Yes. Despite my warnings that it would weaken her

further, your mother nursed that boy as her own along with you and your sister. A house full of babes was the safest place to hide him so I could track Maverene. But she was always just ahead of me."

"She had a mirror that showed her things."

Elspeth nodded.

"I thought as much, which is why I cloaked myself. Apparently, it wasn't enough."

"Greydon told me you raised Garreth."

"I did. I came for him when he was barely a year and old enough to be weaned. Yet, young enough never to remember anything."

"So Mother never planned to give Kellen or me away. It was Garreth you were coming for."

Elspeth laughed.

"Your mother would have never let you go. Not even to me. Is that why you're here? Did you believe she didn't love you?"

"No. I'm here for something I left behind. Something Mother gave me."

I led Elspeth to my attic space where I removed the rings gifted to me by the tree. The one Maeve had taken from me I'd found the night Seth died, and I'd taken care to hide it by the chimney with its partner.

"Mother knew long before I did that I was meant to be with Greydon," I said, holding out the rings.

Elspeth studied what I held then closed my fingers over the items, holding my fist.

"The Prince will be relieved to hear this," she said. "He thinks you're trying to run off."

I rolled my eyes.

"He still doesn't believe I will marry him."

"Have you given him cause to believe that?"

I grinned, recalling all that he'd suffered at my hand, some of it intentional, some of it not.

"At every turn," I said. "But I will spend the rest of my days assuring him that I am his and he is mine."

Elspeth surprised me with a hug.

"You and Greydon will do well together."

EPILOGUE

THE HIGHER PITCH OF DAVID'S VOICE WAS ANSWERED BY A low murmur. I smiled, thinking Greydon was already tucking our son in for the night. However, when I pushed open the door, I saw Aftan sitting on the boy's bed.

"I'm glad the bad woman was killed," my son said. "She shouldn't have hurt my mama."

"No, it was wrong for her to do so. And her punishment, though terrible and hard to behold, was just. Always remember to be fair in your rulings."

"Yes, Grandfather," David said. "But what of Auntie Kellen's story. I want to know what happened to her after she ran away."

I thought of my sister and felt a pang. It had been too long since I'd seen her.

Aftan chuckled and leaned down to kiss the boy's forehead.

"That will have to wait until another time. If your mama discovers I've kept you up this late with stories, she'll serve me stewed plums for breakfast."

"I like stewed plums," David said with a smile. "I'll eat yours for you."

Laughing, I pushed the door open further.

"Your grandfather is right about the time. You need to sleep, David."

He pouted a bit and sat up.

"I need to say goodnight to my brother in case another caster comes, and he needs to be hidden away like Uncle Garreth was hidden away."

I moved close to the bed, and David bestowed a sweet kiss to my enormous belly.

"You know that there are good casters, too. And besides, it might be a sister," I said.

"You're right. No caster will want to steal a girl."

The King and I shared a look, for Maeve had indeed done just that.

"To bed, little one," the King said. "And you too, Eloise. You should be sleeping, yourself."

"I was looking for my errant husband."

"Try the door next to your room."

I returned to our suite of rooms and tried the door to the adjoining room. For the first time in months, it was unlocked. I opened it and looked around the room with a growing smile.

"I can claim no part in the making of that," Greydon

said when I ran my hand along the edge of a hand-carved cradle. "But I commissioned it."

I smiled at him.

"It's beautiful. As is everything else in here."

The soft green wall coverings, small wooden toys, and plush rugs were new to celebrate our second child's birth. Greydon's arms wrapped around my waist, and he gently rubbed my back. I leaned into him with a groan.

"That feels so good."

He chuckled.

"I can make you feel better."

I tipped my head back to look up at him.

"I'm sure you can. But your methods keep putting me in this state."

He picked me up and gave a fake stagger.

"How many children do you carry?"

"Don't even tease like that," I said. Barely halfway through my pregnancy, I'd begun to notice my enormity, as well. The thought of carrying twins didn't frighten me, but it reminded me of my sister and made me miss her dreadfully.

"Eloise, I'm sorry," Greydon said, noticing the fall in my expression and rushing to set me on our bed. "I love you without condition. One child or twenty. And we have the best midwife possible."

"It's not that," I said. "I miss Kellen."

"Ah," Greydon said.

"That's it? Ah?"

He gave me a sheepish smile.

"Of course not. However, the longing you feel for your sister is not something I can as easily remedy. She's a kingdom away. If you were hungry, I could quickly fetch you something to eat. If you were in pain, I could summon Elspeth. If you were lonely, I could read from your favorite book for hours until you would know I will never leave you."

"I want to see her again."

"And you will. But not until after this babe comes. It's not safe for us to travel with you in this condition."

I scowled at him.

"You're being stubborn. Why can't we just invite them here? Why must you condemn what happened to her? It's not her fault."

Greydon leaned forward and pressed a kiss to my belly.

"I never said it was. And I could never condemn her for what she's endured."

I hit his shoulder.

"Invite her."

He sighed.

"How will we explain her situation to our son?"

"With words. It was your father who told me it takes love and understanding to rule a kingdom. What better way to teach him than through telling him the full story of what happened to his Auntie Kellen?"

Greydon sighed, his hand sliding up my skirt along my leg. My pulse started to speed up.

"As you wish, my love. I will send out the invitation tomorrow."

I smiled and ran my fingers through his hair.

"Thank you."

"I will always do what I must to bring you joy," he said. "I will never again shirk my duties to you."

And he proved that thoroughly before I fell asleep.

THANK YOU FOR READING DAMNATION, book 3 of the Tales of Cinder! Please consider leaving a review to let other readers know what you thought of the series. It would mean the world to me!

Be sure to keep reading for more information about Kellen's story and other amazing books by MJ Haag.

AUTHOR'S NOTE

It's hard to know what to say after writing this trilogy. Cinderella's story was never one of my favorites mostly because in all versions, she endured so much. And it chapped me that the prince never really did much to "save" her other than to remove her from a life of drudgery. When I started considering writing my own version, I needed to have an explanation as to why he didn't do more. It helped that I had Eloise kick him in the testicles a few times.

Something else I noticed when doing my initial research is the strong parallels between Snow White's story and Cinderella's story. It was almost like they could be sisters...so of course, that's what I did. I can't wait to share Kellen's story. It won't be as dark (at least, I don't think it will be) and will probably be a lot heavier on the romance. I anticipate having that ready next summer.

For now, the Resurrection world is calling to me again.

There's something about those big grey hotties that demands my attention. Maybe it's their lack of shirts... If you haven't yet read that series, keep reading for an excerpt from Demon Ember. You might just like it.

To ensure you never miss a release announcement, follow me on social media or sign up for my newsletter at mjhaag.melissahaag.com.

Until next time, happy reading!

Melissa

CHARACTER LIST

Eloise - *Cinderella* (Twin daughter of Margaret and Atwell).

Kellen - *Snow White* (Twin daughter of Margaret and Atwell).

Margaret Cartwright - Eloise and Kellen's mother.

Atwell Cartwright - Eloise and Kellen's father.

Hugh - A stablehand.

Judith - A housemaid.

Anne - A housemaid

Lady Maeve Grimmoire - Kellen and Eloise's new guardian.

Elspeth - A caster who Margaret knew.

Rose - A caster/enchanter.

Catherine - A housemaid.

Heather - A housemaid.

Aftan - The King of Drisdall

Sevil - The deceased Queen of Drisdall.

Greydon - Prince of Drisdall.

Grimm - A tracker/huntsman.

Cecilia - Maeve's daughter.

Porcia - Maeve's daughter.

Damnation is the final Tale of Cinder, which takes part in the Beastly Tales world. If you haven't yet read the Beastly Tales, you're missing out on a seductively dark Beauty and the Beast retelling. There's character cross over between the two trilogies that you're going to love.

SERIES READING ORDER

Beastly Tales

Depravity

Deceit

Devastation

Tales of Cinder

Disowned (Prequel)

Defiant

Disdain

Damnation

Resurrection Chronicles

(zombies and hottie demons!)

Demon Ember

Demon Flames

Demon Ash

Demon Escape

Demon Deception

Demon Night

More to come!

Connect with the author

Website: MJHaag.melissahaag.com/

Newsletter: MJHaag.melissahaag.com/subscribe

SNEAK PEEK OF DEMON EMBER

Now Available!

Movement next to my window made me jump, and I turned my head. Yellow-green eyes met mine. I froze, afraid to move. My heart felt like it wanted to pound its way out of my chest. He watched me as I watched him. His focus made me very aware that I needed to do something soon. My shaking was only getting worse. If I continued to hesitate, I'd end up dead like the rest.

My knees still pressed against the seat, my feet nowhere near the pedals. I grabbed the wheel and started to swing my legs to the side. He slammed his open hand against the window. The glass splintered and folded in toward me. He reached in, his hand wrapped around my left arm.

I yelped and pulled back, no longer caring about lunging for the pedals. He reached in with his other hand, grabbed me under the right armpit, and dragged me forward. The steering wheel slipped from my grasp. I tried for it once more but missed as he yanked my upper body out the window. I reared back, flailing. His hold under my right arm slipped, and I struggled to pull myself back in. He reached for me again, missed my arm, and grabbed my boob.

He jerked his hand back, and I froze, staring at him with wide-eyes as I hung out the window, pinned in place by his other hand. He reached forward with his free hand, and I put my arm up, trying to protect my neck.

His palm covered my right boob, and he gave it another tentative squeeze. I lowered my arm in shock and watched him pull back once more. His gaze zeroed in on my left side.

"Hell no," I said, renewing my struggles.

As if his first attempt to remove me had just been a test, he plucked me out of the truck and set me on my feet in front of him. He kept his right hand firmly anchored around my upper arm as he lifted his other hand.

My chest heaved with each panicked breath. When his hand got close to my boob, I swatted it away.

He grunted, lowered his hand to his side, and studied me. When his gaze dropped to my jeans, a new panic surged forth. I pulled hard, willing to yank off my own arm to get away from him. He backed me against the truck, limiting my struggles, and proceeded to pat down the front of my jeans.

"No...no...just kill me already."

He stopped patting and sniffed my hair, my ears, and my face. Shock kept me still for most of it.

Abruptly, he let go and stepped back. We stared at each other as my pulse thundered in my ears. What the hell was going on? Was he toying with me?

The truck still rumbled behind me, a possible means of escape if I could just get inside. With the door handle digging into my back, I edged to the left. He put his hand on the door, stopping my progress. I bolted the other direction. He moved incredibly fast, blocking me by the front tire.

With a growl, he turned toward the hood. He raised his fisted hands and brought them down on the hood. I jumped at the sound of metal crunching on impact. He hit the front of the truck again and again, crushing the metal in until the engine clunked several times then died.

I took an involuntary step back. He'd just smashed a truck with his bare hands. I swallowed hard, and it took a moment to realize he'd killed any means of escape. I stared at him, out of ideas and out of hope.

He wasn't even breathing heavily, just standing there watching me. When he saw he had my attention, he reached up and pulled the cord holding his shirt together at his throat. Within seconds, he had the loose-fitting dark shirt off.

I stared at his heavily muscled torso with increasing despair.

He tilted his head at me, then reached up and patted his chest. First one side, then the other. When he reached for me, I cringed back. It didn't deter him. He followed me and patted first one boob then the other before tugging at my long-sleeved shirt.

My brain struggled to process what was happening.

"I don't want to take off my clothes."

He tilted his head again and waited for a moment. When he reached for the cord at the waist of his pants, I squeaked. My reaction didn't stop him from shoving the dark material down far enough to show me his grey package with a penis longer than any human version I'd ever seen. Not that I'd seen many in person.

He palmed himself as if saying "see, this is what I'm offering you" and watched me expectantly.

"No, thank you."

He shook himself again and, in that moment, I understood he was attempting to communicate.

"I-I don't want to play Tarzan and Jane."